Thug Life

**Lock Down Publications and Ca$h
Presents**
Thug Life
A Novel by *Trai'Quan*

Lock Down Publications
P.O. Box 944
Stockbridge, Ga 30281

Copyright 2020 by Trai'Quan
Thug Life

First Edition August 2020
Printed in the United States of America

Lock Down Publications
Like our page on Facebook: Lock Down Publications @
www.facebook.com/lockdownpublications.ldp
Cover design and layout by: **Dynasty Cover Me**
Book interior design by: **Shawn Walker**
Edited by: **Lashonda Johnson**

Stay Connected with Us!

Text **LOCKDOWN** to 22828 to stay up-to-date with new releases, sneak peaks, contests and more…

Thank you!

Submission Guideline.

Submit the first three chapters of your completed manuscript to ldpsubmissions@gmail.com, subject line: Your book's title. The manuscript must be in a .doc file and sent as an attachment. Document should be in Times New Roman, double spaced and in size 12 font. Also, provide your synopsis and full contact information. If sending multiple submissions, they must each be in a separate email.

Have a story but no way to send it electronically? You can still submit to LDP/Ca$h Presents. Send in the first three chapters, written or typed, of your completed manuscript to:

LDP: Submissions Dept
P.O. Box 944
Stockbridge, Ga 30281

DO NOT send original manuscript. Must be a duplicate.

Provide your synopsis and a cover letter containing your full contact information.

Thanks for considering LDP and Ca$h Presents.

Trai'Quan

Prologue

It was almost over, he thought.

As he laid back on his bunk, looking up at the ceiling, there was a fly still flying around. He hadn't been able to catch the muthafucka yet. The annoying little fuck had been flying around now for approximately three hours. He knew it had been three hours because they'd served chow an hour ago. So, it couldn't have been 8:00 yet. The sun was just going down outside. The fly landed on the edge of the toilet and he watched it move, then stop, then move again. He couldn't move because any sudden actions would alert the muthafucka to its intended demise. So, all he could do was watch the muthafucka and visualize its destruction. It must have felt the heat because it took flight again—but it was almost over.

He was in a small one-man cell, with only a bunk, a mattress, sheets and blanket, the toilet, and a locker with a desk and an iron stool. Twenty-three hours a day it was just him and the fly when there was a fly. Most days he killed the muthafuckas, but this bastard managed to get past the watch. He was in the hole or lockdown unit. He'd been in this cell now for four and a half months. But the fly wouldn't make it that long. The only reason it bothered him some much was because it reminded him of a time back when he was still in Trinidad—

He was seventeen-years-old then, just before he came to the states. The muthafucka he'd depended on the most. The muthafucka who should have been loyal the most. Had ended up being the muthafucka that crossed him the worst. In the end, he stood over the body at an old garbage dump site, and as he looked down at the fool who had done bad. He saw several flies swarm over the body. Now, this muthafuckin' fly was bringing back memories—but it wouldn't be too much longer.

He made it to the states seven months later, paid an illegal passage to Boca Raton, Florida. The word was Miami was too hot for any illegal sneaking in, but it really didn't matter where he came in at. Just as long as he was in. From there, he met some Jamaicans who were doing their own thing in Orlando. So, he hooked up with them, starting out as a soldier in their posse. The old Dredd was having some problems with some of his people up in South Carolina. So, he sent him with the crew that went to North Charleston to see about the situation. He was still young, had just celebrated his 18th birthday, and was trying to make enough money to bring his mother and little sister to the states.

In Charleston, they hooked up with the other Dredd's a rude boy by the name of Noel, who was doing big things on his own. He ended up staying with the Dredd's in Carolina and started making some serious money. That money, he sent to his mother and sister. While he was waiting for them to come to the states, the big Dredd had a problem.

He was in jail on manslaughter charges when his mother and sister arrived. Because of his loyalty, the big Dredd set them straight. The lawyer kept him from being charged with murder, that was the best he could do for him.

This muthafuckin fly was getting on his last nerve, it was only a few more months now. He was on lockdown for shanking some fool who owed him commissary. They thought because he talked like them, he wasn't as dangerous as the other Island boys. Shit, he had been in now for nineteen years and some change. The fools thought because he was about to go home after doing so much time, he wouldn't be about his business.

Just like this muthafuckin' fly, he'd eased his hand down and picked up one of his shower shoes. The fly didn't seem to notice.

Whack!

He swung his legs over the side of the bunk and stood up with his boxer shorts and T-shirt on, and looked down at the fly. Every time a muthafucka thought he was something to play with. They ended up on the short end of the stick. Twenty years had gone by and all he had left was his sister. She was twenty-six now and had two kids. They were still young and she lived in Georgia. After his mother got killed, she moved. She still kept in touch with him and let him know there was a place for him to stay when he came home. That was love because it was about to be over.

Chapter One

Broad River Correctional Institution

Columbia South Carolina, 2010

"Alright, Mr. Santos, that about does it," the woman he'd just handed the ink pen back to said. He'd just signed the release papers that were giving him back his freedom. "And here is your bus ticket." She handed it to him.

He looked down at the ticket, then looked at the $25.00 check that went with it. "Is that it?" he asked.

The female officer looked up at him as if his extra words had made him *HER* problem. "I mean, if you don't want to wait on the van to take you to the bus station, it's an eleven-mile walk. You're free to leave if you want to."

He looked down at the ticket again, he really didn't need it. So, he placed it back onto the counter in front of her. "How about you hold on to that. It might come in handy one day when decide you want to escape your own prison."

He clutched the check, turned, and bypassed some other officers as he calmly walked out the front door. Leaving Officer Kelly standing there with a stuck on stupid look on her face. All of the inmates knew her situation. She was actually living in a very small bubble. Because she was pretty and had an alright figure on her. She'd come to work acting like she wasn't another thot like all the other females. Treating the inmates like shit because it seems she was getting more attention in prison than she ever received in her life. In the end, she turned out being the fool.

She'd been slutted out by a group of male officers. Who couldn't wait to brag about her dumb ass to the same inmates they tried to impress. Most male officers knew they stood guard over the very guys they envied. For being the thugs, gangsters, and hustlers, they were too afraid to be. So those male officers sought the male inmates' approval.

About six officers had gotten her drunk at a party and taken turns running through her ass. It was a complaint she tried to file

9

that eventually got her the job in I.D. and property. She picked up the ticket and looked up at the back of the inmate. She glanced around and made sure the Lieutenant wasn't around. Then slid the bus ticket into her pocket, just in case.

***

When he stepped outside of the prison, he squinted his eyes. Having maxed out his sentence while in the hole. The brightness of the sun's light seemed to be just a bit too much for him. After a moment his eye's adjusted, then he looked around the parking lot. The sound of the horn blowing drew his attention as the grey and white 2009 Denali pulled up to where he stood, with the passenger side door to him, the window came down allowing him to look inside.

Francis smiled when he saw the woman looking back at him from the driver's side.

"You gon' stand there and smile like a cat? Or are you going to get in?"

He'd just turned thirty-nine-years old, which made her exactly twenty-six now. The only pictures he'd seen of her had been whenever he had the chance to use someone's cell phone and he saw those on her Facebook page.

"What's up with all of da bright colors?" he asked as he opened the door and climbed inside.

Everything his sister had on was pink, even her hair was dyed pink.

"It's my new style. You like it?" Woman asked.

Woman was her nickname, she tossed her head so that her curls could bounce.

"Yeah, it's all you." He smiled.

"Speaking of styles." She twisted her face up, looking over the cream-colored prison clothes they gave him upon his release. "Yeah, we gon' have to do something about that."

She then put the SUV in gear and drove out of the prison's parking lot. It wasn't long before she ended up back on Broad River

Road. Woman punched something into the truck's GPS. He didn't say anything, Francis was thinking about their Moms. He remembered telling ole man Lester while they were playing Chess one day. That the first chance he got, he was gon' see about the little punks who got away with her murder.

"Nah, Young nigga, you've got that shit all wrong," the older man said. *"Yo ole lady wouldn't want you to be no fool. You been in this bitch a long time. I'm quite sure she'd want you to get on your feet. And enjoy how life is supposed to treat you. Not rush back to visit."*

While in prison, there weren't a whole lot of people that he would open up and talk to. Because he'd seen so many funny style niggas' in prison. There was an evolution that he watched from the very beginning of his sentence. It used to be, all the solid niggas stuck together. They recognized that the C.O.s, wardens and other staff were the enemies. Niggas D'ed up on their law work, sat down when the food wasn't right, or the staff wasn't treating them right. Wrote their Grievances and lawsuits etc. They stuck together, solid niggas,   but as the hands of time turned, he watched as two things happen to change all of that.

The first was in part due to society. They started to lock up more and more of the youth. Giving them a whole lot of serious time. These young niggas were given more time in prison then time to mature. Meaning they were still kids, being sent to a grown man's world. In the 1980s Nancy Reagan started her *war on drugs* campaign. Then Clinton entered the picture with the *Get tough on Crime theme*.

So, he watched as more and more kids came to prison. At first, it wasn't so bad. Just young victims of a targeted society. Then, out of the blue air, Francis watched them give jobs to the welfare class of young women. That is what fucked the entire prison system up. Granted, these women needed jobs and had to work somewhere, right? However, what you had was a whole lot of young uneducated stupid niggas.

You put young, childish minded women over them. He'd watched it happen. Niggas at one point would be down to go against the common enemy, the correctional officers, were now selling one another out for just a little attention from one of these women. That fuckery started, and all of the *Real* nigga statuses went out of the window.

***

At Ridgeland Fashion Mall, his sister dropped a good $1500 on a decent hookup. She wasn't rich, but her kids' father made sure she wasn't hurting for anything. As Francis walked through the mall he was aware of several women checking him out.

"*Nigga, don't get out there and get you a nothing ass bitch. Because if the bitch ain't about nothing. Then she ain't gone help you be nothing,*" one of the lessons the old man in prison offered.

Some older convicts would take the time to really educate the young. Then there were the old men who had many hidden agendas. From being homosexuals to being cowards who claimed gang affiliations, and used the young gang bangers to do bullshit.

"I would have thought, you'd move to Atlanta," he said. "From what I hear about it being the spot for blacks now. So, why Augusta?"

"Solomon picked Augusta, he knew some other Dredd's that were already there," she explained. "Besides, you'll probably like Augusta better than Atlanta. They got too many booty boys up there now."

this caused Francis to laugh. "Booty boys everywhere these days," he said.

They rode in silence for a while, listening to what was being called Hip Hop. He couldn't relate to half of it but kept his opinions to himself. This being what the youth were into these days, 90% of these young niggas was emotional as fuck. You disagree with them, they twist their faces and say you're hatin'.

"So, what's in Augusta?" He finally asked.

"Thug Life!" she stated.

***

Francis had no idea what *Thug Life* was. Other than having heard the late rapper Tupac stress it so often. He naturally assumed this was what she meant. In truth, the prison had suppressed most of the foolishness that was once inside of him. Now he was more focused, now, he had a greater vision. He thought as he drifted off to sleep, enjoying the ride.

***

The house his sister lived in was off a street called Olive Road. A nice white house with a small front yard and three bedrooms. Since both of her kids were girls, she was able to place them in the same room. This allowed her to give him a room.

"I've got some ganja. You wanna smoke before I go pick the girls up?" she asked.

"Yeah, one. Where dey at?" he asked.

Woman's real name was Lisa, but not too many people really knew her by it. She came around and sat on the couch, pulling the coffee table closer. Then she poured a good portion of a Ziplock bag that she had. The weed was red and green and knotted in lumps. So, she had to break it into pieces and separate it as best she could. Then she pulled out a box of Vanilla flavored blunts and began to split several of them open. Then she emptied the tobacco out into a large pile at one end of the coffee table.

Francis sat on the other end of the couch and watched as she rolled the blunts like a true technician. Then without wasting a moment, she pulled out a lighter and set fire to one end of the blunts. She paused and inhaled taking a deep breath. He could smell the vanilla flavored scent mixed in with the weed smoke. It did smell exotic. Woman hit it again, drawing deeply. Then she passed it. Having not smoked any serious weed in twenty long years, Francis started coughing and choking like a newborn baby.

"Damn." She laughed. "I thought you was smoking up in that place?" She laughed once more as she received the blunt when he passed it.

13

"That shit they be smokin'—" He choked. "That shit ain't really all that strong. I think they call it loud simply because the smell is loud." He coughed again. "But the high ain't worth shit really," he explained.

Accepting the blunt back, he noticed that this weed didn't have the same smell as the weed in prison. For one, it didn't smell *Loud* as they called it. Yet, what his sister had was several times stronger.

"You know yer boy, Mishna, is also in Augusta these days," she mentioned.

She'd already told him that on the phone about four months ago. He guessed she didn't remember. So, he held his tongue and didn't say anything as she brought the subject up.

"He heard how good Solomon was doing. So, he moved his thing from Jacksonville, Florida up here. Plus, I think he's been in contact with, Big Dredd, too."

He didn't really doubt that Big Dredd Noel was doing a bid in the Feds. After been hit with the Rico Law a few years back. Even from inside the Federal Prison, the Big Dredd still had a lot of dealings going on in the streets. At the moment though, Francis was thinking about Mishna. In Hebrew, his name meant *To Study*. He hadn't seen Mishna since he left Trinidad, with him being the oldest by one year. He had, however, heard that Mishna was able to find his own way into the states after he'd ended up in prison.

"So, what's he been up to?" he asked.

"Doing his own thing. Here." She tossed him her Samsung. "His number's in there."

He scrolled through the memory until he came to the number. He pressed it just as she got up and walked to her room. There was a Jamaican song for his ring tone.

"Yooo, what up?" Mishna answered.

"That boy Ruuude," Francis said.

"What, who dis?"

"It's me star, Rabbi," Francis stated using his old street name. The one everyone knew him by. They once called him *The Priest*.

"Get da fuck outta here! Where you at, Rude?"

"I'm at Lisa's lab. She picked me up this morning when dem people let me out," he explained.

"Whoa! She stays on Olive Road, right, the white house? Yo, I'ma swing through and pick you up. Give me like twenty minutes," he said.

Then the call ended. Francis sat there, high and thinking about the last time he'd seen Mishna. That was right after he'd killed Ganja. He'd never told her he was the one who killed Ganja. Instead, he made up a story about finding him already dead. As a *rule*, Francis *never talked about the soul he had to put to rest.* To him, it was like calling down bad energy on yourself. Not long after he killed Ganja he found his way into the States.

He shook off those memories and waited for Mishna to arrive.

***

Francis was standing outside when Mishna pulled up in all-white Range Rover Sport Evoque. It boasted a nice set of 24-inch Pinnade chrome rims. He watched as the truck stopped in the middle of the street, placing it directly in front of the house. He watched as his old childhood friend jumped out looking like a rapper.

Mishna, at the age of thirty-eight, stood a good 6'1-inches and had a sepia, reddish-brown skin tone. He looked like he weighed about one-hundred, ninety-four pounds. He was wearing a pair of faded jeans a Nike t-shirt with the latest pair of Jordan's.

"Whadda up, Rude?" Mishna came around his truck and met Francis halfway.

They shared a long-lost brotherly embrace.

"Damn, nigga, I ain't seen you is so long," Francis said, then laughed. "Shittt, you done grown up. No more skinny, nigga," he added.

"Me." Mishna laughed.

He stepped back and looked Francis over carefully. Seeing the Tru Religion jeans, Roca Wear shirt and pair of Airmaxes.

"Nigga, you da one looking like da Incredible Hulk's lil' brother," he stated.

At a good 6'2" in height, Francis spent most of his time in prison working in the kitchen and working out. All his other free time was reading books. Especially those written by *Trai'Quan*. His favorite was *Omerta Black*.

"But, yo' check dis. Tell Woman you rockin' with me tonight. Nigga, we got a lot of catching up to do," he said.

Francis turned to the house and he went to do just that. She scolded him a thousand ways before he left, but he wasn't planning to get in any trouble.

***

Francis accepted the blunt from Mishna as he maneuvered the Range through traffic. They'd just turned off Milledgeville Road. A song by *Jada Kiss* was pumping out of the speakers. However, the music wasn't turned up too loud, because Mishna was talking.

"So, Woman took you shopping and got you a few outfits huh? It's a'ight, but yo' put this in yo pockets." Mishna held out a large roll of bills. Francis accepted, held it up, and looked at it. Thinking it might be ten grand.

"I'ma come through tomorrow, too. Snatch you up, and we gon' hit the Augusta Mall. I'ma drop like two or three more of those on you. Ya, hear me, Rude?" Mishna asked.

"Yeah, but listen star." Francis pocketed the ten grand. "You ain't gotta break yo' pockets to show a nigga you got love, Rude."

"Nah, it ain't that. Nigga, I been eating good out here," Mishna told him. "I've got this trap spot, it's over next to the hood called Sunset. Yo' it's a million-dollar trap, Rude, them white folks keep beefin' wit' them, project niggas. They done tried to rename the area several times. At the end of the day, it's still gon' be Sunset. While all that be going on, Lucky Street and every other trap street around it be jumping.

Francis didn't know shit about Sunset or Lucky Street. His time here in the states had been spent mostly in Florida and South Carolina. Yet, he figured he needed to be listening, and learning what he could about the city he was now in. Especially with this being where he was about to live.

"So, what you moving—crack, heroin, or something else?" Francis asked out of curiosity.

"Bruh, let me put you up on some serious game. Right, now, the crack hustle is putting a lot of niggas under the chain gang. Oh, I'll move it, if it comes through my hands. And it does from time to time. But the truth is, I'd rather sell a nigga his own snow. Let him cook his own shit up. They give you less time for the snow then they do for the rock," Mishna explained. "But right now, Rude," he continued. "The streets seem to be flooded with two things, Ecstasy and pain pills. Muthafuckas is buying that shit like it's candy. I've got a little ganja mixed in the hustle. Yo, you hungry, Rude?"

Francis watched as he turned into a Krystal's, found a spot and parked, then they got out.

"Like I was saying, Rude. The only niggas out here selling crack is them thirsty ass, stupid niggas. Them ones looking for that head rush money. A patient nigga, a smart nigga who ain't trying to go to prison—"

They reached the door to the establishment, Mishna pulled it open and held it for him. "Niggas like me, we trying to keep our names from getting hot in these streets."

Once inside they saw a small line of people, with only about three people in front of them. So, it wasn't a long wait. When they did reach the counter, Francis was just about to say something when the dark-skinned girl behind the counter receiving orders looked up.

"Hey, Baby, I didn't know you were coming by," she said.

"Yeah, my nigga just came home. So, I scooped him up. Ayo, Rude, this my girl Angel. Angel, meet Rabbi."

"Hi," Angel spoke. "So, what can I get you two? Yall look like y'all smoked out." She laughed.

"Thug Life," Mishna stated, then made his order.

Francis also made an order, then they took their food and found a table in the far corner.

"So, that's yo girl?" Francis asked.

"What? Oh, that's one of them. I've got another bitch at this other spot called Cheeda's. You know a nigga gots to eat." Mishna laughed.

They began eating their food. Francis was trying to figure out if he wanted to put his hand into this cookie jar. He didn't really want to ask Mishna for a handout. Shit, the nigga had just blessed him with ten grand and was gon' spend another twenty on him tomorrow. That was a nice piece of change, but then too, the nigga hadn't sent him a dime while he did that twenty years. Yet, it wasn't like he owed him shit. Plus, he still hadn't put the call into the Big Dredd, yet. There was no telling what he was gon' say. So, he decided to hold his tongue and see what fate had in store for him.

Chapter 2

He was awakened by two little girls who looked just like his mama. One was eight-years-old while the other one was ten-years-old. The oldest one was named after his mama, Lakeisha, while the youngest was named Tameika. After they introduced themselves, he got up and went to take a quick shower. He'd hung out with Mishna until it was late last night. They'd just rode around, with Mishna showing him all the popular areas. Sunset, Ginning's Holmes, Southside, and Ole Savannah Road which they called D.S. Richmond Villa, Shirley Avenue, Woodlake, Pepper Ridge, and Fairington.

Most of which he said niggas hung out in because of the women. He also showed him some of the hottest clubs. Hollywood, Creams, the Soundtrack Dirty South, and Cloud 9. There were so many different spots that he couldn't remember them all. They hadn't stopped at any of them. Mishna explained that most of the hoods were beefing with one another. So, unless you knew someone in those neighborhoods who would green light you. It wouldn't be safe getting caught in one of them.

When he exited the shower, he took the time to look at himself in the mirror over the sink. He hadn't been able to exercise since about the time he killed the fly. So, he knew it was long overdue. In his room, after he brushed his teeth. He dressed in a pair of Roca Wear jeans, a Phat Farm T-Shirt and Airmax sneakers. He kind of wished he'd gotten more than one pair of shoes, but it wasn't his money.

He found Woman and his two nieces sitting at the kitchen table eating breakfast.

"A'ight, so, what tastes good?" he asked.

"Cereal!" Tameika stated as a fact.

Lakeisha nodded. "Yep! Chocolate Cocoa Puffs, too," her statement caused Woman to shake her head.

At the moment she was texting on her phone, but he grabbed a bowl and poured some Cocoa Puffs into it.

"Wait a minute, I thought all Cocoa Puffs were chocolate?" he asked.

"Well, yeah, I just didn't know if *you* knew that," Lakeisha said.

Francis sat at the table and began eating with them. "And, why wouldn't I know that?" he asked.

"Well, you've been in jail. I heard all they gave y'all to eat was bread and water, no real food," Lakeisha said.

"I have to have cereal," Tameika put in. "Bread and water just don't sound too good."

Francis would have laughed, but he didn't. Sometimes it was good when people on the outside thought prison was worse than it really was. It would keep them from wanting to visit one day.

"Big Dredd said to call him when you get settled in." Woman looked up from her phone. "He said to tell you not to rush yourself either."

He suspected she had mentioned that he'd been hanging with Mishna, but he didn't say anything. He'd see what Big Dredd had to say later.

***

Mishna came through just before noon, Woman had already taken both girls to school. Then said she had some other things to take care of. She said Solomon would be home sometime this weekend, they hadn't met yet. The ride to the Augusta Mall was one spent listening to the music. He assumed Mishna had done most of his bragging yesterday. But just as he thought it, Mishna spoke.

"So, what I'm saying is this," Mishna was continuing his pitch from last night. Trying to get him to come work with his crew. "I could set you right, Rude. Give you a nice package. Let you work it over on Lucky Street. Shit, in a month you'd have your own whip."

"That all sounds good, but I just got word. I'm waiting to hear from the Dredd tonight. Ain't no telling what that's gon' be about," Francis told him.

"Word, come on, they got some nice shit in here."

They parked and exited the SUV. Then Francis followed as Mishna led him into one of the men's clothing stores. Once inside Mishna began going through some of the latest fashions. Francis was just looking because it wasn't like he had to worry about the prices. Plus, he'd been gone twenty years, and most fashions changed daily. There were only a few styles that you could always count on. Shoes usually made what you wore stand out.

"That probably wouldn't look good on you."

Francis cocked his head to the side at the comment. He looked around, then became aware of the female store clerk. At first, he thought she was a white girl. Until he looked beyond her pale skin complexion and began to see the slightly wide nose, the shape of her eyes, and cheek structure. Those, he knew, came from *black* genes somewhere in her bloodline.

"You're talking as if you really know men's clothes," he made the statement bold.

The girl smiled, showing off her pretty whites. He also noticed that her hair was sort of kinky with a touch of red. She almost put him in the mind of the girl from that TV show Girlfriends, named Lynn.

"Let's just say I know clothes," she shot back. "I pick out all my boyfriend's clothes."

"A'ight, so what do you think *would* look good on me?" he asked.

She gave him a serious, concentrated look, then turned and began selecting various clothes. Francis saw that she defiantly had a black woman's ass.

"How about we try these on?" she said.

***

Jasmine was thinking that this guy was defiantly fine. But when he removed the shirt he had on she saw his muscles defined in the tank top he wore.

'*Damn!*' She had to glance around to make sure she hadn't spoken out loud.

She had him try on several *Dolce & Gabbana* shirts, picked out some jeans by Sak's, and threw in some colored dye *Timberlands*.

When she finished, he did look brand new as he checked himself out.

"Thanks—Mrs. Uhhh," he said.

"Jasmine." She showed him her name tag. "And its, Miss."

"Oh, my bad, I didn't even see that. I'm Francis." He held his hand out.

Jasmine shook it. "No problem, Francis. And maybe we'll see you again," she said.

What she really meant was *and maybe she would see him again*. She had to catch herself before the words slipped out. Especially since she already had a man. Hell, she was only looking. She watched all the way as he took the clothes to the register. Where his friend paid for them.

Damn, looks like he might be one of those Homo-Thugs. Damn shame, too. The nigga is just too fine. Jasmine shook her head.

***

"I saw you getting your swerve on, Rude," Mishna said as they exited the store. "That lil' bitch thinks she's all that. She fucks wit this Blood nigga named Brian. He a dope boy up on the Hill," he explained.

"Oh, yeah, I thought she was a white girl at first. I didn't know she was ghetto fabulous." Francis laughed.

Realizing that Mishna felt some kind of way by the girl showing him attention. He was thinking, Mishna must have shot at her before.

"Nah, she a good bitch."

They reached the Range Rover and got inside. Mishna picked up the conversation as he drove. "She ain't one of these hood bitches who be fucked out. This nigga *B* met the bitch at Augusta College. I used to fuck with a bitch name, Connie, who does all the dope boy's girlfriends weave. She told me 'bout the hoe," he explained.

Not that Francis was even giving her that much thought. Instead, he was thinking about making this call to the Dredd later tonight. Having just gotten out, he knew how shit on the inside went.

Noel probably had his phone put up, and only pulled it out after Administration left for the day. Because Woman said he was supposed to call after 7:30.

***

"That nigga, Mish, Po Bitch. What up, Thug?"

Francis watched as the brown-skinned nigga who opened the door greeted Mishna. This was supposed to be his trap house. He wanted to show Francis the operation.

"What up, Thug? Ayo, this my nigga, Rabbi. Nigga, I grew up wit' back on da Islands. Rude just did a duce. Yo' Rude, that's Shoota Boy and the Po Bitch playing the PlayStation is Yard King, they're my lieutenants," Mishna explained as they stepped into the house.

Francis was somewhat catching onto the Augusta slang. Everybody was called *A Dirty Ass Nigga* or a *Po Bitch* which he didn't really understand. From outside, the house didn't really look like much. But once you stepped inside the whole house looked like new money. From the PlayStation 2 connected to the 64-inch screen TV, which sat next to an audio system that looked serious. To the crystal, glass coffee table that sat in the middle of the room. Around it, there were two large black bean bag chairs. Behind it was an even larger bean bag couch.

"Come," Mishna said as he led him further into the house.

They bypassed a few rooms, but Francis noticed there were also a lot of guns throughout the house.

"You not worried about the cops wit' dem guns?" he asked.

"Nah, neither one of them young niggaz has a criminal record. And dey under seventeen. Dem guns is clean, no bodies on em, but look here."

They'd just reach the kitchen, where there was a homemade lab set up.

"We make everything in this muthafucka," he bragged.

"But like I told you, Ecstasy is the main business, right here. This right here is the acid drop." He showed Francis a tub that held

23

acid inside of it. "Da cops come Thug and dem dump all the drugs in the tub. I can get dem off on the guns. But the dope will get even a young nigga a court appointment."

He didn't have to tell Francis, because he knew that was the truth. He'd seen *too* many young niggas coming in as he was getting ready to go home. For either drugs or shooting somebody. The judge didn't show favoritism.

***

"I saw you checking out Mr. Muscles."

Jasmine looked across the top of her silver Lexus GX460, with Zyoxx rims on it. She saw Keidra getting into her Infiniti EX35. Keidra worked in the store, too, but was a well-known hater. Jasmine figured she hated on her because of her color and her being biracial.

"Wasn't nobody lookin' at no muscles," she stated.

"Uh-huh, if that's what you keep telling yo' self. But hey, I would have looked, too," Keidra said.

Jasmine was quite sure she had looked. Either way, she waved and got into her vehicle. She wasn't about to lose any time and energy on Keidra. Jasmine could never understand why black women viewed her as a threat. It wasn't her fault that her mother was white. But she was still black because her dad was light-skinned. Either way, she knew that other then her complexion and light, hazel eye color, everything else came from the black side of her. She was twenty-three-years old, with no kids, standing 5'9 and weighed 134 pounds, all of it was athletic because she was on the school swim team, which contributed greatly to her 34-24-39 measurements.

She didn't act like a white girl, but she didn't act ratchet either. Her music of choice was Hip Hop, but she had an ear for the old stuff, too. *Nas, Lauren Hill, DMX,* and *Missy.* She still couldn't figure out why so many darker-skinned women hated her, she knew some of it had to do with her boyfriend Brian. Jasmine wasn't stupid, she knew Brian was like nearly every other man in the streets.

A dope boy, hustla, playa, and a gang banger. He was popular in the streets. Nearly every woman on the Hill kept his name in their mouth. It took a lot for her to not feed into their drama. Out of all that, the one thing she could say, he hadn't let any of his bullshit come her way. Even if she did suspect that he was trimmin' around, although she couldn't find any proof of it.

***

"Yooo,' who dis?"

"Rude boy, Rabbi, Peace what up, Dredd?"

"Boy." Noel laughed. "It's good to hear your voice. Lisa told me you've gained some weight. So how you doing?" he asked.

Francis gave him a play by play of everything he'd done since coming home. To him, Noel was like the Father he never got to know. Even with it only being a short time he'd spent around him. He always liked how the older man handled business. There were very few loose ends when Dredd made a move.

"Okay, so Mishna has been showing you some love right?"

"Yeah, but yo' it ain't where I really wanna be. You know me Dredd. Ain't much done changed in twenty years. I'm still an independent nigga. I like to have my own," Francis explained.

"Yeah, yeah, I know," Noel said over the phone. "And truth is, I still feel like I owe you for that trip you took."

"Listen, bruh, that was all love," Francis told him.

Because Noel had taken care of his family for him. Even now he suspected the old Dredd was still giving Woman money when she asked.

"Right, love is love, I know that. But here's the thing, I could use a little assistance out there. Someone reliable, and it's really a small thing," Noel told him.

"Whatever you need, Dredd. I got you, bruh," he said.

"Don't worry about it. Here's the deal," Dredd told him.

Noel began explaining to him what he needed him to do. Francis listened and processed the information.

***

Mishna didn't know what to make of this nigga yet. In a way, he was feeling like prison had changed Rabbi. Because he didn't really act the same. The Rabbi he knew was full of energy. Always looking for a come up, and extremely dangerous if it was necessary. The nigga he'd shown his trap to and spent the past two days with, didn't seem like the same nigga. The old Rabbi would have jumped at the chance to be down with an operation like the one he had going on.

Then again, Rabbi said he was waiting to see what the Big Dredd had to say. The only thing about that was he knew that the Big Dredd no longer dealt with hard drugs. In fact, he didn't think Noel dealt with the drug game at all. So what Francis would get out of that he didn't know.

***

Brian was sitting on the hood of his blood-red Mercedes Benz SL-Class convertible. Talking to one of his little bitches on his phone when Jasmine pulled up and parked directly behind his car.

"Look baby let me go ahead and call you back later. This nigga J-Dogg just pulled up."

He ended the call just as Jasmine exited her car. They had an apartment further up towards Washington Road. In a nice gated community, where the only crime noticeable was an occasional domestic dispute. At the moment, he was parked in front of the apartment complex that was called Hampture. Where his boys trapped out of several of the apartment. A couple of their girls were Rubies, the title Bloods used for their girlfriends.

"What's up, baby, you good?" He kissed her as she walked up.

"Yeah, I'm good," she said. "I just stop by before I got home. So, what you got going on?"

He had to admit, though, the bitch was still looking good even wearing her work clothes.

"I'm just out here watching my scraps earn their stains. Shiittt, you know how I do."

Jasmine looked around and saw the activities. She knew that nearly every dope boy out there was one of his lil' homies. Brian was the Big Homie, and at 29 he'd been G-Shine before he came to Georgia and started putting it down. He was originally from the Bronx, New York.

"Well, you coming home later tonight? Or are you sleeping out here in these streets?" she asked.

"Nah, I'ma pull up. Just let me get some of this check out of the spot first. As a matter of fact, since you here—" He turned and called one his scraps over. "Yo' run on inside and get them dineros for me. And don't be taking yo' time either."

"You gon' have him give it to me out here. I thought you didn't do business out in the open?" she said.

When the kid came back out, Brian had him go put it in her ride, since the driver's side window was down.

"Look, ma, no hands." He held both his hand up.

"A'ight, well I'll see you at the house."

She gave him a kiss, then turned and walked back to her SUV. Like always, Brian and a few of his lil' homies had their eyes glued to her ass cheeks. All of them loving the way it moved as she walked. Jasmine got back in her ride and pulled off.

***

Unknown to either one of them was the unmasked Mazda CX-7 parked further up the street. So, they didn't know or suspect that the FBI had been taking pictures of Brian as he watched his trap. They'd just taken quite a few pictures of the young drug dealer as he placed the money inside of her SUV.

"Do you wanna pull it over?" the agent sitting behind the wheel, looking plain in normal clothes asked.

"Nah, it's probably just money," the one in the passenger seat taking the picture said. He made it a point to snap a few more pictures of her tag as she drove off.

"We'll pull her sexy ass in when we make the case on this chump. Who knows, she might even roll over on him," Camera guy said. "I'd like to see her roll over alright. All nice and naked."

He licked his lips, already imagining having a taste of something like that, even though, it was something he'd never get. Mostly because he was a *nobody* and he looked and dressed like a *nobody*. Other then him being an F.B.I agent, that's exactly what he was, a *nobody*. Nobodies ever got to be with women like that. The closest they ever came to it was when they went to a strip club and spent their hard-earned money. On those nights they got to feel like somebody, but in the end, it would cost them $200.00 or better.

"How much longer the big guys want us to take pictures? We've already got him with what looks like his plug," he said.

Talking about the pictures they'd taken about a month ago. In them, Brian was with a middle-aged Cuban from Miami, Florida, that they assumed was Carnelito. They'd been trying to get the infamous Carnelito whose rumors spoke loudly for years. Every time they thought they had him, some other Cuban would step in and take the charge. The Cuban in the picture, they knew was a wealthy Cuban that owned businesses in Miami and other areas of Florida and he was politically connected to someone.

"Won't be too long now," his partner said.

He too was wishing that they could get the Cuban. But as always, this Cuban made very careful moves. They never had anything solid on him. Only the people he was seen talking to and that wasn't enough.

Chapter Three

Three Weeks Later

Francis was thinking it was a good thing the rental car came with a GPS. Because he wasn't sure if he would have been able to find the address without it. The last thing he wanted was for the police to pull him over, he didn't have a license yet. Lisa said she would help him get one. She knew a girl who worked at the place. But that would have to be when he got back. When he reached Buford South Carolina, he could remember some of it.

A lot of things had changed in twenty years. The GPS directed him to a house located not far from the beach. He could see the lighthouse as he stepped out of the Nissan Sentra Sedan. In the house's driveway, he saw a Cadillac ATS-V Coupe, a Porsche 911 Turbo Carrera convertible, and a black on black Lincoln MKX. While he stood there, admiring the vehicles the door to the house open. When he looked up, he could see a Jamaican standing in the doorway holding what appeared to be an M-4 assault rifle that had a cooler on the barrel.

"What up, Mon? You da, Rabbi?" he asked.

Francis somehow got the feeling that if he wasn't the Rabbi. He wouldn't be leaving this house today, and with it being secluded, you couldn't see the house from the main road because of the trees.

"Yeah, dat be me," he said with his accent.

"Oh, yeah?" the Jamaican asked. "You da, Death Priest huh?" He looked around, then his eyes looked over the car. "And, who sent you, Mon?" he asked.

"The Big Dredd, Noel."

The Jamaican with the gun nodded his head.

"Come den."

Francis sighed, then started towards the house. He hadn't been afraid of anything a day in his life. But he was cautious because he knew these types of people weren't known for playing games. They didn't take chances either. He knew for a fact, he could die just as easily as he'd pulled up.

***

Once inside of the house he saw several other Jamaicans. Who were all sitting around smoking ganja as if it were a marijuana holiday or something. As he moved into the room, one of them held out a large blunt. Francis took it and noticed that the guy was older, somewhere in his later years. But he smiled when Francis accepted the blunt.

When he brought the blunt to his lips and hit it. Amazingly he didn't choke this time. The Jamaican he'd received it from nodded his head. Over the past three weeks, he'd been smoking a lot with his sister and her boyfriend Solomon who was also Jamaican born. So his lungs had adjusted by the time he made this trip.

The ganja was so good he nearly got lost in it. He was about to take another toke when the curtain that was made of beads parted. He saw a woman carrying a baby on her hip wave for him to follow her. Francis handed the blunt back to the old head. Then he turned and followed the woman. She led him down a long hallway. At the end of it, there was a screen door. Stepping through the door he found himself standing out on a back patio. Seated at a table with a crockery made of ceramic in front of her, was a beautiful, brown-skinned woman with very long, blonde dreadlocks. He didn't know what was inside the pot, he suspected he knew what it meant.

"You de Rabbi dat Noel sent? You know why you here?" she asked.

The woman was still looking into the crockery. She hadn't even looked up at him yet.

"Not really," Francis said. "He said she would give me something and explain what to do."

Now the woman looked up and into his face. "I Ms. Sheba." She tapped her chest. "But before I give you what Noel tell me to give you. I need you to kill a man for me."

He almost asked her to repeat what she said but thought better of it. Common sense said if she asked him to do her a favor. Then it must be important and this was Noel's sister. He nodded his head and watched as the woman, Ms. Sheba smiled.

***

He was told that he had to wait until later that night. When the moon was up high in the sky. Then one of the Jamaicans that had been sitting in the living room smoking, drove him to a beach house in the Porsche.

"Der two people in der—both of dem must die," he explained to Francis.

Then Francis pulled out the Glock 22 that he'd been given for the job. It came with an extended sound suppressor attached to the barrel. As soon as he stepped out of the Porsche, he inhaled the night air. The breeze coming off the water made the air seem sweet. He took a moment to look around carefully. The house was one of the beach condominiums and because they were designed for privacy as well, there weren't any close neighbors to them. He turned and began walking towards the house.

He could see there were still some lights on inside. Moving with both care and extreme silence. He made it up onto the back patio. He moved to the glass sliding doors and saw that they were locked. Looking through them he was able to see a couple sitting on the couch, in front of an opened fireplace. They appeared to be drinking some champagne. He stepped back he glanced around carefully.

Then he aimed the gun at the glass door. He squeezed the trigger and kicked at the same time, which caused the glass to shatter. As he stepped inside the white woman jumped up and started screaming. He pointed the gun and squeezed shooting her twice in the chest. He watched as she froze then fell to the floor. Francis then turned to the white man who hadn't made a sound yet. The guy didn't even seem surprised to see him. It was almost as if he expected this.

"Out of curiosity, who are you anyway?" Francis asked, watching as the man sighed.

"I was his lawyer," the attorney stated.

"So, you knew this was coming?" Francis nodded his head at his own statement. He now understood clearly why he'd been sent to kill the man.

He squeezed the trigger, shooting the lawyer in the face. Then, after the body fell. He moved forward and unloaded the rest of the clip into both bodies. Francis dropped the gun like he was told, then turned to leave. He didn't remove the latex gloves until he was back inside the Porsche. Neither he nor the Jamaican spoke as they rode back to the house, words weren't needed.

***

Ms. Sheba was standing outside in the driveway as they pulled up. Francis noticed that the rental car was gone. He was just about to say something when he noticed her holding out a set of keys to him.

"De Lincoln is yours. You keep when you get de chance look under de canvas in de back. That's what Noel give you. De car I give," she explained.

Francis looked down at the keys in his hand. "A'ight, so what do I do now?" he asked.

Ms. Sheba had already turned to walk back into the house, but she stopped and looked back. "It's both ole pay and new pay. Old from twenty years ago. Big Dredd say your loyalties unquestionable. And de new is for de jon you just do," she explained. "Oh, and Big Dredd says, you stay out of trouble."

He watched as all the Jamaicans turned and followed her back into the house. After the door closed, he realized it was over. He turned to the MKX and pressed the alarm button on the key chain. When he opened the door, he found the sales slip lying on the driver seat. He picked it up and saw that it was made out in his name, meaning the SUV had been sold to him. He got inside and started it. It was a long drive back to Augusta.

***

He found a truck stop where he pulled in to get some gas. Once he'd pumped it he went inside to pay. He grabbed a bag of chips and a Sprite soda. Then asked the guy behind the register if there was a bathroom. The guy said it was around behind the store. Francis pulled the MKX around back and saw that it would be too hard for someone to see him. He went around to the back of the SUV and open the hatchback. Inside he saw the large black canvas. Then after another quick glance around he lifted it.

What he found was what looked like a lot of compressed ganja. He couldn't say how much but knew it was a lot. Big Dredd had said he didn't personally deal with heavy drugs anymore. Francis also saw the wrappings of money that lay alongside the marijuana. Even that looked like *a lot* of money. Francis replaced the canvas the way that it was. He opened the bag of chips and began eating them as he looked around. The ganja didn't smell. So, he assumed it was vacuum sealed. Which meant he shouldn't have a problem driving with it. He just needed to drive careful. He would still need to get that license, especially now that he had his own ride.

***

Brian was in the process of counting all the money he'd made this month. It would have been two times more if Carnelito's people weren't so worried about the Feds following him around. The way Brian saw it, if they were gon' come, then they were gon' come. There wasn't anything he could do to stop them. This was why his thing was to make and hide as much money as he possibly could before they came. He was preparing himself for the cold winter. Shit, it was too late to get out now.

Nevertheless, he had half a mill stashed at his grandmother's house up in Fayetteville, North Carolina, and another quarter mill at his Auntie's house here in Augusta. That, along with the $170,000 he'd just made. That wasn't counting Carnelito's re-up money which he had set off to the side. He picked up the cigarette that was sitting inside the ashtray. Then took a puff off it, Jasmine was at work, so he wasn't worried 'bout hearing her lip. As he looked around the apartment and saw the nearly quarter mill he'd spent on furniture.

He couldn't see why she threw a fit about him having drug money in the house. It wasn't like he was stupid enough to bring the work home. But shit, it was the work that paid for everything. How a bitch wanted to live the good life, but not be reminded of what it took to get it. He just didn't get it. Just as he was thinking this, there was a knock at the front door. Brian stood up in his boxer shorts and T-shirt, leaving the money and the Smith and Wesson model 29 .44 lying on the kitchen table.

"Yeah, who it is?" he called out.

"UPS, we have a delivery here," a female voice said.

Looking out of the peephole he saw a white woman with black hair wearing a UPS uniform holding a box. Probably something Jasmine done ordered, using his drug money. He smiled as he thought that and unlocked the door.

"Yeah, what is—"

He tried to ask but was assaulted by the F.B.I agents as they pushed into the apartment. They had both guns and badges out, screaming at him.

"Freeze! Get down on the floor! F.B.I. get down!"

"Ain't this a bitch," he said to himself as they slammed him face-first into the rug.

He was just thinking that some shit like this could happen. Well, at least he did have a good lawyer on retainer. All he had to do was make a call.

***

Jasmine was having a bad feeling all morning. Something just kept telling her that today wasn't a good day. But she couldn't see what the problem was, then, as she was speaking with one of the customers, she looked up and saw the woman and two men enter the store. They were wearing the Navy blue windbreaker with the letters DEA on them. They also wore hats and had their guns on display. When the manager rushed to see what was going on.

Jasmine knew three things instantly. The first, she had just lost her job. The second, they were there to arrest her, and lastly, her father was going to be pissed.

***

At Phinizy Road, the new Richmond County Jail. Jasmine was booked and fingered printed. Then allowed to make her one phone call before they placed her in a holding cell. From what she'd been told. They caught Brian with a whole lot of money at the house. There were also several guns that she wasn't aware of, but no drugs. They placed her in the holding cell after the call, she was with several other women. Most of them looked like they were on drugs. The others looked like prostitutes. She found a seat somewhere in the back and sat quietly. Not even bothering to try and socialize with the other women. She eventually began to think about what would happen next. She didn't have a record and had never broken the law. So, maybe it wouldn't be so bad.

There was an orderly outside sweeping the floor. She watched as a folded piece of paper was slid under the door. One of the other women picked it up and read the name.

"Anyone in here name, Jasmine?" she asked.

"Yeah, me," Jasmine spoke up.

The woman walked over and handed her the note. It was from Brian. Apparently, he was over in another holding cell. In the note, he was pleading with her to take the charges. While still stressing about how much he loved her, but wanting to ruin her life. She balled the note up and began to cry. The door was open twenty minutes later.

"Ms. Grant, your attorney is here to see you," the female officer said.

"Damn, girlfriend, you must be a boss bitch. It ain't even been an hour yet," one of the prostitutes said.

Jasmine didn't speak, she stood and followed the officer to a conference room. Once there the officer opened the door and let her in. Then she really broke down in tears as she saw her father.

Assistant District Attorney Lloyd Sullivan Grant. Jasmine fell into her father's arm and cried even harder. She was ashamed and knew he was about to make all the pain go away.

***

After listening to everything his daughter told him. Lloyd left the room. He instructed the officer to leave Jasmine in there. Because he was well known at the jail, they didn't even question him. Especially when they finally realized that jasmine was his daughter. The F.B.I kept a small office at the jail. When he reached it, Lloyd tapped on the door, then poked his head inside.

"Ray, can I have a word?" he asked.

Raymond Conlyn was the senior F.B.I agent over most of their cases, he knew the ADA well. He raised his hand and waved him in, motioning for him to have a seat.

"Listen, Lloyd, we had no idea that this was your girl. We don't know a lot of you people's families. For that I'm sorry," he explained.

Lloyd smiled. "I understand, but here's the thing, Ray. Just what is she being charged with?"

"Shit, we ain't got nothing on her. There might be a picture or two of her receiving some money. But hey, this guy was her boyfriend, right? He's the one we want."

"Yeah, I'm aware of that," Lloyd said. "The bastard even had the nerve to ask her to take the charges."

"Whoa, look, Lloyd," Raymond began. "I'm throwing everything we have on your girl away. Prints, pictures, everything. I'm even going to let you take her with you. We don't even need her for the case. We've got enough on this guy as it is—" He paused and looked in Lloyd's face. "—but if she does that. Man, I can't let her go, I'm sorry."

The ADA understood, so he nodded.

"Don't lose any sleep on it, Ray." He smiled. "She's not taking any case for anybody. You have my word on that."

"Well, then, we're good here," Raymond said. "But hey, I'm sorry she had to lose her job. Man, like I said, my guys didn't know who she was," he apologized again.

Lloyd sighed. "Do you need her for anything else?"

"Nah, we're good. Just tell her we're sorry about the job," FBI agent Conklyn said.

***

"What am I going to do about my apartment?" Jasmine was in the process of saying.

They were standing out in the parking lot next to her GX460, which the FBI released because it had been paid for by her father. Not with drug money. It had been the gift he gave her for college.

"The apartment is gone," Lloyd said. "It's part of their investigation now. But follow me to my office and I'll write you a check. Enough for you to find another nice place."

"Yeah, but now I owe you money," she pouted. "And I still don't have a job. How am I going to pay it back?"

"Well, there is still *that* job," he stated.

"Oh, my God. How can I be a cop now? I've been arrested. My prints are on file as a possible criminal," she pointed out.

He was silent for a moment. "Tell you what," Lloyd said. "If you take the job at the jail, I'll have all that erased. But you've got to give me at least eighteen months on the job. Or they won't do it for me," he lied. Not bothering to tell her that everything was already being removed.

"Well, let me find an apartment first. Alright?" she said.

***

"Big Dredd gave you all that?" Lisa asked.

Having just walked into the kitchen and saw the large compressed two tons of marijuana. That was still packaged the way he received it. Then there was the money, all of it was on the table.

"Yeah," Francis said. "He said for me to stay out of trouble. You know weed don't carry as much time as coke. But that's still a lot of ganja," he pointed to it.

"True, but it'll sell fast. I could hook you up with some of the girls where I get my hair done. Them bitches love to talk, but I know most of their niggas either sell weed or smoke it," she said.

"Just as long as my name don't hit the street. That in itself would be bad," he said.

Then, as if he'd just remembered something else. "Oh, he gave me a Lincoln MKX, too. So, I need to get that license as soon as possible."

She laughed. "I was wondering if that was a rental parked outside," she said. "But I've got you. My girl Makeba works at the place. I'ma go call her now."

She left to go make the call, leaving him still sitting there looking at the ganja and money. There was approximately $175,000 from what he'd counted. He planned to spend at least half of that getting his own place. He was still thinking about how Mishna had his trap set up. He could see something like that, but not on the same level, and defiantly not in the hood. He was going to find a way to sell the ganja. But he was going to do it without being labeled a drug dealer and he was going to need a job.

The only problem with that was he didn't have any real job skills. In prison, he discovered that he had a passion and ability for writing. He'd written a few short stories and let niggas read them. He had even written one of those urban novels but had lost it during a riot.

Francis was thinking, he could get himself a nice computer and do some writing. Although, that wouldn't be seen as a real job until he could get two or three published. Then he was a convicted felon. Even if he wasn't on any paper, he still couldn't be out hanging in the streets. Things had changed over the years. The young guys out in the streets now were trying to make a name for themselves.

He couldn't see letting one of them kill him to get famous. Nor did he intend to kill some mother's baby. So, yeah, he needed some type of job. Even if it was a bullshit job. He needed something to keep the cops off his back, too. He also needed to open a bank account. Those were the smart things to do.

Trai'Quan

Chapter Four

Francis found Mishna in the middle of Sunset. Not actually the middle, but on Tobius Court where it seemed like every dope boy in the projects was standing around. At the moment they had something like a hood version of the UFC going on. There was a lot of betting and cheering going on. He saw that there were two kids in the middle of the court fighting. One of the dope boys was even refereeing.

"Po Bitch, bob, and weave nigga!" Mishna was in the process of shouting when he walked up to where he stood.

"What it is, Rude?" he asked.

Making his presence known, Mishna held a hand full of money just like several of the others he saw.

"What up, Star?" he spoke. But his attention was still on the action in front of them. "Ohhh, get up nigga. Get up!" he shouted.

The one he appeared to be backing had gotten knocked down, but he did get back up. Francis had learned two important things since he'd been out. The first was a lot of people called Augusta the boxing capital of Georgia. He'd already known who Vernon Forrest was and how he made Augusta look good in the ring. After seeing him beat up on Sugar Shane while he was in prison. That was before some guys had murdered him in Atlanta. The Augusta's boxing club was nearly a legend. Many of the women who had kids that got into trouble would suggest that their son's go visit the boxing club. It was also an outreach program for the youth.

The second thing he'd come to learn was that Sunset Holmes was considered the actual Heart of Augusta. When he'd asked Mishna about the whole *Thug Life* movement. It turned out it didn't have as much to do with the rapper as he thought. Both Thug life and LOE, *loyalty over everything* represented all the streets, niggas, in Augusta. LOE was the movement that began as a means to keep Augusta niggas loyal to Augusta. Since there were so many gangs nowadays. From the way, he understood it, in prison and juvy Augusta niggas wasn't supposed to go against one another. Thus, *Loyalty Over Everything* on the streets. Thug Life was all the jack boys, killas, and dope dealers the toughest of the tough.

This project, Sunset held one of the biggest reputations in Augusta for thugs. Their reputation went all the way back to the 60s and 70s. As far as he understood that is, it could have been longer. But there was thugs all over Augusta.

The fight ended with Mishna losing his money. Francis stood by as he paid off all the people he'd bet.

"What up, Rabbi? Been a few days, Star. You good?" They fist bumped.

"Yeah, I'm good. Had to see what Big Dredd wanted," he said, noticing the way the statement drew Mishna's attention.

"Yeah, so, what up?" he asked.

Nonchalantly Francis said, "He gave me a truck and some pocket change to play with. Then told me to stay out of trouble. Keep out of the streets."

He didn't feel that it was necessary to tell him about the ganja. He damn sure wasn't going to bring up the thing with the lawyer. That had always been his number one rule. He *never* talked about how many heads he'd put to rest. Only fools bragged about what they did. A nigga who wanted to be seen was a nigga who'd always been overlooked.

"That's all?" Mishna looked disbelievingly. "He no give you no work. Nothing? Just a truck and some bank."

Like everyone else from his past. They all knew that Francis had gone to prison on a call that was made by Big Dredd. So, Mishna was looking to see him get put on proper.

"You know he don't fuck wit' the drug game," Francis said. Feeling like he didn't really have to. "But shit, he took care of my Ma, and Woman when I wasn't der. So, to me, he made good. Me and him, we good," he explained.

"Yeah, a'ight," Mishna said hesitantly. Francis didn't like the way that sounded. "What kind of truck did he give you?" he asked.

"A Lincoln MKX, 2011 next year model," he said.

"Okay—okay, that's tight. How much bank?" Mishna asked.

"Damn, nigga, you checking my pockets now? I thought only pimps checked bitches about their paper?" Francis said and watched as Mishna checked himself.

"Where you parked at, Star?"

"Up the street from your trap house."

"Come on, let's go look at yo' shit," Mishna said.

***

"Cynthia, I'll need you to show Ms. Grant how to run the desk. It's her first day here on the job," the older white woman said.

She smiled as she walked off and left Jasmine with the short, heavy-set, brown-skinned woman. Jasmine listened as she explained what she would be doing. Which was accepting the money and giving receipts to discharge the tickets as people came to pay for the tickets they'd received. It didn't seem hard and was, in fact, easier than what she'd done at the clothing store. She didn't have to wear a police uniform except for twice a week. She was working at 401 the old jail on Walton Way.

She had received some messages from Brian. It seems they hadn't told him everything that happened. He didn't know that she hadn't tried to take the charges for him. Instead, he was told that there was too much evidence against him and that none of it implemented her. No one told him that her father was one of the state's ADAs. Since his case was federal, they would never cross paths.

As Jasmine was simply left looking like a woman scorn. As if she were the one done wrong. She continued the check her father gave her. She'd found a nice two-bedroom townhouse behind the Danial Village Shopping Plaza. That brief run in with the law had changed her life. She vowed that she would never be placed in handcuffs again.

***

"Listen, Dude," Mishna said as he sat in the passenger seat of the MKX and rolled the blunt while Francis drove. "A nigga wasn't trying to check yo' pockets. I would never treat you like a bitch, bruh. You gotta know me and you, we like fam. Your moms was

like my moms. Yo' pain when you heard she'd been murdered—
Rude, that was my pain, too."

Francis glanced over at him in silence as he drove. He was remembering the last time a nigga used that type of argument on him.
That was the nigga he left to the flies that day in Trinidad.

"I was just trying to make sure you alright, Star." He lit up the
blunt and inhaled deeply. "Sure, Noel, he looked out for the family.
But Star, this nigga is still a multi-millionaire. The Feds didn't take
all his shit. Because they couldn't find all of it. Bruh—" He passed
the blunt over to Francis.

Francis began hitting it, feeling disenchanted at the moment, but
he didn't speak his thoughts.

"I just feel like you should be getting a gold spoons for twenty-
years of loyalty, bruh. That's all, no disrespect intended," Mishna
said.

Francis continued keeping his thoughts to himself. Because he
really didn't feel like Mishna had a right to feel some kind of way.
He himself hadn't done a thing for him in twenty years. Woman
hadn't said that he broke bread with the family. So, who was he to
be questioning the only nigga who had?

***

Over the next two weeks, Francis found a nice townhouse and
got his license. He spent most of his days held up inside of a motel
room. He broke the ganja open and had the whole building lit up. In
fact, the weed could be smelled all the way down to the gas station.
But he knew that was because there was so much of it. He'd had to
break the motel manager and two of the cleaning ladies off, to keep
them quiet. Then, one of them, a Puerto Rican female helped him
out.

"Papi, why you no burn you a tire? It's what my Hector do when
he have stinky stuff," she said.

"Burn a tire?" He was vexed.

But she stood there and nodded like it made perfect sense. Then
she explained, "Yeah, you get you one of those trash cans that the

bums be using. Put an old tire in it and then set it on fire. The tire burn for a while. The rubber makes big black smoke. And it smells really loud, but don't let the policia catch you setting the fire."

He'd done just what she explained. It worked and he also met Hector who was Mana's boyfriend. They became business associates once he smoked a joint of the ganja. Hector brought a pound as soon as Francis finish bagging it up. He'd purchased one of those air sealing machines so he sealed all of the bags tight. Hector made sure to get his cellphone number too.

***

He met Young Castro through Raine. Raine was a dark-skinned female that was 5'5" and extra thick in all the right places. She was one of Woman's friends and was a year older than Woman, Raine was twenty-seven. When Woman pulled her aside and invited her to the house. She didn't think anything until they were in the parking lot. Where Woman asked if she wanted to buy some weed. Woman said she didn't want the gossip girls in the beauty shop to hear her business.

"Are you selling this?" Raine asked as she looked at the Ziplock bags. That he'd brought from his house. "Because my babies' daddy can help you get rid of it."

He looked up at Woman, who nodded.

"His name is Young Castro. He sells Ecstasy over on the Boulevard," Woman said.

"Every now and then he'll sell some ganja. But that's only if it's some good shit," Raine said.

He gave it to her, it was three days later, and he'd forgotten all about it. When he got the call on the new Galaxy he'd brought he was confused at first.

"Yooo' you the kid wit' the smell good?" A voice asked with a thick New York accent.

"What, smell good? Aye, Star, who dis' playing on my phone?" Francis asked.

"Yooo, my bad, son. You a Rasta. Yo' peace, my girl Raine, she came through with some nice smelling shit. And it tastes good, too. She said you might be trying to drop a few double extra larges."

Then he remembered. "Oh, yeah. You, Young Castro, right?"

"No doubt, no doubt. So, we gon' get up or what son? I'm interested."

"Yeah, but not on the phone, though," Francis said.

"Can you meet me at the Dairy Queen's on Peach Orchard Road?" he asked.

"Just say when, Pa," Young Castro said.

"Shit, I'm pulling in it, right now. I'll be here for a second. Just pull up," he told him.

***

"War of the wooden Solider, Cee Cipher punks couldn't hold us, a thousand men rushin' in not one nigga was sober."

Francis was eating a vanilla, chocolate chip cookies, and candy Blizzard when the black Escalade SRX pulled into the parking lot beating down the block with the Wu-Tang playing. He couldn't help but admire the 26-inch Panther rims that were on it. He watched as the truck pulled up and parked next to his MKX. Then Young Castro got out. He couldn't have been more than nineteen maybe twenty. He was about six-feet-even and possibly one-hundred, ninety-five pounds. What made Francis suspect this was him would have been the dreadlocks, and he was dressed like a New York nigga. Wearing the large baggy jeans and a 4XL Iceberg shirt. He was also wearing a pair of green Wallabies.

'*Definitely New York*,' Francis was thinking as he entered the building. He held his hand up and flagged Young Castro to the table where he sat.

"Yo,' what up, Pa?" Young Castro asked.

Pa being a New York phrase that was common amongst the older five percenters. It was like saying son and meant something like respect towards someone that was your senior. The two men first bumped.

"Hold up, before we talk. B.I., I'ma get me one of those mutha-fuckaz."

Francis smiled and shook his head as the younger man went to the counter to get his own Blizzard. From what he could tell, he liked Young Castro's energy. A lot of the brothers he'd met in prison who were from New York were official. That wasn't to say that *all* of them were 100. When Young Castro returned, he sat across from him and started eating.

"Wifey told me you was good people. Plus, I know yo' fam. Woman, solid," he said, then ate a couple spoons of his ice creams.

"Basically, I'm trying to get off this ganja without putting my face on it," he explained. "I move in the shadows. Not trying to be seen."

"Yeah, yeah. Yo, you been around some up top niggas, huh?" Young Castro stated,

"A few here and there," Francis said.

He knew it was the movie the shadows thing that got this attention. Most playmaker would move from the shadows. Behind the scene, he learned that from some of the New York guys in prison. Some even said that that's what made the mafia so powerful. By the time people realized they were doing something. It would be too late to do something about it.

"But, yo' Pa, it's some good shit, too." The younger man said between bites. "I wouldn't have pulled up if it was that thirty-minute loud shit. Sometimes that shit lasts an hour. But you've gotta keep smoking that shit just to stay high. Now, this shit wifey pulled out the other day, I smoked one vanilla sun and guess what."

He paused to eat another spoonful of ice cream.

"The shit had me seeing pink hearts, yellow moons, and blue diamonds. And the shit smells good," he stated.

Francis couldn't help but laugh. Nearly, every New York nigga he'd met had a way with explaining their reality.

"A'ight, so tell me. How much can you move?" he asked.

Then he watched as Young Castro thought about it.

"Son, you talking ounces because Pa it's gotta be more than thirty-two of them. Because once niggas start smoking the shit they gon' want two and three at a time. So, I'ma have to get like pounds of it."

Then it was Francis turn to pause in thought. "How about we do it like this?" he began. "My sister says your good people. So, how about I sell you the two, right now. But seeing as I brought five pounds with me. And I'm not trying to keep riding around wit' it. I'ma front you the three and you call me when you get that bank."

He watched as Young Castro paused with the spoon almost to his mouth. His eyes looked on him.

"What, nigga get the fuck outta here," he said and watched for a sign that Francis wasn't serious.

"Yo' Pa, you serious. Nigga say word!" he said.

"Word, but here's the deal," Francis explained. "I can pretty much keep you on deck, but—"

"But what, come on Pa. Don't play wit' a nigga emotions and shit," Young Castro said.

"Two things, one, nobody knows my name, nobody knows my face. I'm not coming to your trap nor am I hanging out in any dope spots. Which means we meet wherever I say we meet," Francis said.

"A'ight, a'ight, is that both things?"

"Naw, the second thing is, you gon' have to buy at least five pounds, whenever we connect. Anything less than five and I'm not listening. But this front on the three, you should be about to get the streets jumping."

He watched as Young Castro pulled his phone out. "No doubt and as soon as I have wifey come pick em up. I'ma take you to a strip club, Pa. Yo' we gon' chill. What up, you down?" he asked. Then he spoke into his phone. Telling Raine to come get the smell good from Dairy Queens.

Francis was thinking why the hell not? He didn't have anything else to do.

***

The strip club was located down on Broad Street. Francis couldn't remember the name it. At the moment he sat next to Young

Castro and they were smoking a vanilla-flavored blunt. While they were doing this, there was a thick, brown-skinned, slanted eyed stripper up on the stage. Francis had never been to a strip club. He definitely wouldn't have thought he'd be hanging with a nigga like Young Castro. Sitting inside of a strip club watching a woman shake her ass. The whole thing was a new experience.

There was even a point where some guys at another table tried to get the girl to come over to their table. But Young Castro put an end to that.

"Look, Ma—" He flashed her a whole fan of hundred dollar bills. All of them spread out so she could clearly see that they were hundreds and not ones. "Go ahead, Ma—take one." The girl reached out and plucked one of the bills. "Matter of fact, take two, my man's think you're sexy."

The girl smiled at Francis as she took another bill. After, that, she wasn't about to go dance at no other table in the club. Young Castro explained that most niggas came to strip clubs with rolls of ones, and made the girls work extra hard just to earn her money.

"Most of them niggas is crab's yo'. Niggas who acting like they rich, but they ain't," he said.

Then he beckoned the girl closer. She squatted down placing her spread thighs in front of them, with her whole *life* on display for them.

"Yo', you smoke, Ma?" he asked.

"If it's just weed, I don't smoke nothing mixed," she said.

Young Castro passed her the blunt, Francis wasn't mad. While she squatted there, he noticed that she had a tattoo of a popsicle on the inside of her thigh. It was definitely holding his attention.

***

Later that night, they met up with the girl whose name was Iesha. Since she'd gotten off, they smoked another blunt with her out in the parking lot. Then eventually they ended up at a motel. Young Castro spent most of the time hitting her from the back. While it seemed liked she was enjoying giving Francis head. After they both busted. They smoked another blunt. Then they switched positions. Francis suited up, then began fucking her from the back while she turned her head sideways and sucked Young Castro's dick. Before the night was over. They'd both fucked her twice and gotten head twice.

It was early the next morning when they brought her back to the club. Because she had to get her Subaru Tribeca. But she also took the time to program her number into Francis' phone. Young Castro said his girl would go through his. But they did say that they might come back and watch her dance again.

***

It was 6:30 a.m. when they pulled up to the IHOP and went inside. They both ordered large plates of pancakes and beef sausage with eggs. Neither one of them ate pork. But they drank several cups of coffee. Trying to shake the sleepiness and the weed off.

"Ayo, Pa, this is on the one," Young Castro said.

"You a cool ass nigga. Ain't that many heads down here I chill wit, but if you ever wanna hook up and go fuck some bitches, yo', call a nigga up."

***

She knew that this was going to be the part she would hate. Jasmine thought as she rushed to get dressed. Having to get up this early to go to work. Her last job was manageable when it came to the time. She stumbled out of the door, with her shoes in her hand. It was 7:10 and she had to be at work at 7:30 on the head. Which meant she had to skip breakfast. Only being able to stop for a cup of coffee at one of the gas stations on her way to the jail.

As she pulled her GX460 out of her driveway and into the street. She was the person who'd moved into the condo across from her pulling in. He was driving an MKX which she thought was a nice ride. However, other than the fact that it was a guy, and he blew his horn. She couldn't tell anything else. Because she was in a rush. She wasn't trying to get a ticket on her way to work. How stupid would that look, with her receiving the money people paid?

***

Francis waved at the GX460, but he wasn't able to see the person driving it. He'd been living in the neighborhood for almost a month and never had a chance to meet any of his neighbors. Mostly because he wasn't home during the day.

"I'm so tied up on my own. I'm so tired of being alone, won't you help me, girl, just as soon as you cannn—"

The music was pumping out of his sound system as he opened the door and stepped inside. As a rule, he always left the music on. Even when he was home because it established its own ambient sound. He'd pretty much borrowed from Mishna's concept with how he had his trap house furnished. Not too heavy, just enough to make his own concept work. Since this was a condo, that gave him more space. So, with the bean bag couch and twin bean bag chairs. He had them spread out in the living area with the couch in the middle.

A black glass coffee table sat in front of it. Then there was the 70' something inch plasma screen TV mounted up on the wall, connected to it was the PS2 and a nice stereo system sat under it. Directly behind the couch was his solar pex gym set. As a personal item, because he saw that he was looking out of shape since he'd come home, he couldn't have that.

Francis undressed and walked upstairs to take a shower. Still thinking over the deal he'd just made with Young Castro and the time they'd just spent. He no longer had to worry about moving the ganja now. Young Castro would be doing that, which meant he could focus on finding him a good job.

Yeah, he needed a job. There wasn't any way to get around it, even it meant accepting a job at one of the fast-food places for a while. Because he would really need to open up a bank account. The money form the ganja would be coming in on a regular pretty soon. He thought about Mishna. He really didn't know what was going on with him. The fact that he'd heard many stories of how shiesty niggas got in the game.

However, envy was an emotion that he made a habit of dodging every chance he got. Because he knew it would make a person sour. As a mental reminder, he made a note to ask Dredd if there was some bad blood between him and Mishna, which he really couldn't see. Big Dredd didn't waste time on petty issues like that.

As he finished his shower, his thoughts suddenly turned to vision of the biracial girl from the store. His dick hardened as he wondered what she might be up to. Then the ole prison mindset took over and he began to, as they said in prison, *squeeze one-off*. Remembering her from that day.

Chapter Five

"I'm the Dow Jones of rap and my stocks is high, and it never was all love so stop the lies. Muthafuxkaz'll blow yo' brains out and watch you bleed. The same niggas that you trust let em watch yo' seed, you gotta dead niggas cause money don't stop the greed—" - Jadakiss 'Kiss of Death 1999.

Four And A Half Weeks Later

Francis turned the music down as he turned onto the street where he lived. Tired from work, he just happened to find a medial job at a used car lot. One where he had to wash all the cars and kept the whole lot clean. He wasn't quite sure if he got over on the old Jew who hired him or not. He was only making 7.00 an hour, and the guy knew he was a convicted felon. He'd had to explain the circumstances of the case that sent him to prison. But he didn't have any real skills, and at the front door to 40. What else could he expect?

Because of the job he was only clearing a little under $500 every two weeks. But he didn't see a need to cry about it, all other things considered. He had about 800 in the bank from the two checks. Since you couldn't put more than ten thousand into a bank without drawing the FBI's attention to it. He'd only placed 9 thousand into the account from the money he received on the ganja. Using Big Dredd's help, he now had a Cayman's Island bank account, set up under numbers instead of his name.

That account held close to 300,000. Big Dredd had been showing him how to hide his money. So, that he'd always have access to it but the IRS nor the Feds could touch it.

He pulled into his driveway and started to get out. It was also at that same time that the GX460 swung into the driveway across from him. This being the very first time he'd ever pulled up at the same time as the other person. But the only thing his eyes as the woman exited the SUV was the police uniform.

Damn, I live across from a cop, he thought.

At the same time, he ducked his head slightly and threw his hand up in a friendly wave. But made it his business to go ahead and enter his condo. *Ain't that a Bitch*! Even if Young Castro and Hector had put a sizable dent into the two-ton. He still had a lot of fucking weed stashed inside of his pantry.

***

"Damn, I know that guy, don't I?" Jasmine said to herself.

She waved back but also noticed that he'd sort of ducked his head a bit. He must've been looking at her uniform as he entered his condo. She hadn't gotten a clear look at him. But there was something vaguely familiar about the guy. She gathered her things, then went into her condo. Still hating the fact that they'd moved her to central booking two days ago, which was both a gift and a curse. It was a promotion in both rank and pay. One that she suspected came once everyone figured out who her father really was.

Also, the fact that he was next in line to become the Chief District Attorney. The current one was being considered for a judicial appointment. No one wanted to start out on the wrong foot with the next possible Chief District Attorney. That wasn't a smart play. Because there wasn't any telling when they would need something from DA's office. Jasmine had learned quickly that favors went a long way on this type of job. The curse was, she now had to wear the uniform five days a week.

"No wonder the guy ran into his apartment. Probably thought I was going to arrest his ass," she said as she stepped inside.

She placed her Gucci bag on the couch and immediately began removing the uniform. She pressed a button on her answering machine as she walked by on her way to the kitchen. Wearing only her Liz Claybourne laced bra and panties. There were only a few messages. Most, she knew would be in her voicemail. She hadn't even checked the messages on her iPhone yet. They weren't allowed to take their cellphones into the jail unless they were detectives or lawyers.

Standing in front of her refrigerator, drinking a Michelob Light. She still couldn't shake the feeling that she knew the guy across the street. '*Or maybe I'm just being horny*,' she thought. Since Brian, she hadn't been with anyone, and since she'd had this job. It seemed that she hadn't been approached by any real men lately. Oh, there were plenty of cops that asked her to go out. But they weren't nearly her cup of tea. Sad to say, but she had a thing for *Thugs*.

***

Mishna was pissed and mostly because he couldn't understand why it bothered him so much.

"I know this nigga workin', I just can't prove it," he said to himself as he pulled up to his trap house.

He wasn't talking about the job Rabbi had at the used car dealership either. In his mind's eye, he was trying to convince himself that Rabbi was hustling. He parked his truck, then got out. When he went inside, he saw Shoota Boy and Yard King playing Tekken 3. But his mind was on something else. So, he didn't stop to kick it. He just nodded and rushed into the bathroom to piss. This nigga Dirty 'A' kept saying that he was seeing Rabbi at the strip club he owned. Every time he saw him, the nigga was with this New York nigga Young Castro. But Mishna hadn't seen Rabbi with the young nigga. Nevertheless, every time he tried to pull up on the nigga he was busy or something.

When he finished pissing, he flushed the toilet. Then he turned to the sink and washed his hands. When he came out he went into the bedroom. Moving the SK semi-automatic rifle off the bed. He fell across it, still thinking. The whole business was getting on his nerve. He'd never like them New York niggas in the first place. Every time he looked around it seemed like them niggas were doing too much. Shit, he was glad when he heard the news. That the Feds had pulled up on the lame-ass nigga, Brian. Now that nigga was doing the most.

All his high profile flexin' and shit. Them niggaz was really making the streets hot. Especially them Blood niggas. Always acting like they had a point to prove.

'*Nigga, this ain't California*',' he always thought.

This nigga Young Castro wasn't no better. Nigga had the whole 8th and Grand Boulevard lit up with this new ganja he had. The thing about that, if he didn't know the dreadlock wearing muthafucka had a reputation for having some good weed. He would have sworn this nigga Rabbi had his hand in it. But nah, the nigga wouldn't lie to him, would he? Other than the MKX, the nigga wasn't flexing like he had big money. Even if he did, it would be hard to tell. Because he pretty much suspected that Big Dredd would give the nigga anything he asked for. That was fuckin' with the nigga. Shit, he was, Rude Boy, too.

"I know what I'ma do—" He sat up and dug into his pocket to pull out his phone.

***

Two full hours had gone by. Jasmine had taken a shower and was debating on what she wanted to eat. But even that was put on hold as she hung around the front windows trying to see if this guy would come out. Her whole aim was to get a good look at him. However, it didn't look like he was coming out anytime soon. So, she sat there frustrated for about ten more minutes. Thinking about how boring her life had really become. To the point that she was sitting by the front window stalking her neighbor. On top of all that, it was a Friday evening, and she didn't have anything better to do.

Finally, she couldn't take it anymore. Wearing her apple bottom shorts, Baby Phat top, and wedges by Prada. She got up and grabbed her keys.

"I'ma do this before I lose my damn mind and nerves," she told herself. Then open the door and stepped outside. She turned and begin walking across the street.

***

Francis was listening to *Keyshia Cole's Woman to Woman* as he exercised in his home gym. He now had everything that he needed to keep in shape. Given the fact that he was about the see his fortieth birthday. He knew he had to keep himself in shape. Which was why he'd just finished doing a rep of 25s on the bench when someone knocked on his door.

He damn sure wasn't expected, anyone. The only person who even knew where he lived was his sister Lisa. Either way, he stood up and grabbed a towel. He'd been working out for the past hour and was soaked with sweat. His tank top didn't have any dryness to it at all. But there wasn't any time to run and freshen up. Whoever it was would just have to take it as it came. He walked to the door and didn't even think to look through the peephole and see who it was before he opened the door. Instead, he just reached for it and pulled it open.

Then, for a moment it seemed like time stopped as the two people stood there looking at one another. Then they both smiled.

"Francis right?" she asked.

"Yeah, and your Jasmine?" he said. Trying not to remember his action in the shower not to long ago. "How did you know where I lived?" he asked.

Then he leaned forward and glanced outside. He didn't see a car. Nor did he see the way her eyes lusted over his chest when he leaned.

"I didn't, you sort of waved when I came home and I thought you looked familiar," she said.

He looked across the street to the GX460.

"Ooohhh, you're the cop? I thought you sold clothes at that store in the mall?" he said.

"Yeah, I lost that job right and you can thank my ex for that one," she told him. "So, all this time you've been living here? And it looks like I've interrupted your work out, too."

"Uh, not really." He glanced behind him and sniffed the air, to assure that it didn't smell like ganja. "Hey, you wanna come in?"

He stepped back, holding the door open. Jasmine stepped inside and as she did, she admired his decorative style. Definitely a bachelor's spread.

"I've only been here a little while." He smiled as he closed the door. He saw the way she looked around.

"Oh, and I'm not really a cop either," she stressed. "My dad got me a job at the jail. I work in booking. So, I don't arrest people," she explained.

This allowed him to breathe a sigh of relief.

"That's, uh, good to know. But, uh, is your dad a cop?" he asked.

"No, he's a lawyer," she said. Not really lying. "So, uh where's your friend?" she asked.

"Who, Mishna?" he asked and gave a confused look. "Why would you think he'd be here?"

"I guess, I uh—assumed."

Francis busted out laughing as he realized what she really meant.

"You thought we were gay?" He laughed even harder.

"Well, it looked like he was buying your clothes. I just thought you know." She hunched her shoulders. Also feeling embarrassed at the same time.

Finally, Francis caught himself and was able to stop laughing. In a way, he could see her point of it. "Nah, I'd just come home from prison. Mishna was just showing some love. Because he didn't break bread while I was in," he explained. Then laughed again, he couldn't help it. "Neither one of us are twinkies, "he said.

Then as an afterthought, she added, "What about—you know, crazy as drama queen girlfriends. Because I'd hate for one to pull up and claim I'm after her man."

"Nah, you good! I'm single. But look, would you like to go out and get something to eat? I mean all you gotta do is step back over there and make sure everything at your condo is cool. Let me take a quick shower and throw on some clothes. You game?" he asked.

"Sure, besides, I don't want to wear this anyway. It's just house wear," she said.

"A'ight, well I'll pull up over your way in about thirty minutes."

***

"That bitch Raine said she don't know where the nigga be buying his shit from."

Mishna listened to what Inez was telling him. Inez was the bitch that owned the hair salon up in the Southgate Plaza. Her salon was famous because it was where all the dope boy's girls went to get their hair done. Inez was that nigga Juggernot's bitch. Everybody suspected that he set her up in the salon. They thought he used it to clean his money. Juggernot was the third-largest local dope boy in Augusta. Some people even assumed that the nigga was a millionaire. Mishna didn't know about all of that. All he knew was, from time to time, like all these other dope boy's girls. Inez would call him when she wanted to get her back blown out. The bitch had some good pussy, too.

"And you don't know? Yo' nigga ain't heard shit?" he asked.

"If you just tell me what you trying to find out, I'll know what I'm supposed to be looking for," she said.

That was one of the things he hated about the bitch. All these hoes loved to gossip, but this bitch Inez just knew *everybody's* business. The bitch was worst then the fucking Feds. Always had both of her fucking ears to the street.

"I just need to know if he's getting his shit from Woman's people," he said.

"Oh, you mean Francis, her brother? Nah, I doubt it. If I ain't mistaken, not too long ago he was trying to buy some ounces. That's probably how you heard his name in all of this gossip," she explained.

'*Damn*,' he thought, because he'd been sure. "Are you sure about that?" he asked.

"Yeah, I'm sure. I was doing Tiffany's hair when Woman asked Raine if her nigga still had some more of that good smelling shit. She said her brother was trying to buy two ounces. And that was after Young Castro came out with the shit he selling now. So, I don't think that nigga got no hookup," she explained.

"Yeah, a'ight," he said.

Mishna ended the call before she could hit him for some dick. He wasn't even about to smash the bitch for some information that wasn't worth shit. So, Rabbi was buying Ganja from this nigga, Young Castro. He still didn't feel the situation. It seemed like the nigga didn't want to come spend his dough with him. Even if his shit wasn't as good as what this nigga Young Castro was pushing. Nah, he wasn't feeling that shit.

***

"So, what do you think?" the agent behind the wheel asked.

They were sitting inside a Toyota Venza that was smoke grey and had deep tinted windows.

"I don't know, I can't really get any good pictures from this angel. And it doesn't look like he's moving reckless," the agent with the camera said.

"Yeah, but if the tip we got is good. Then this guy is doing a whole lot more then what it seems."

Lucky Street wasn't an easy street to run surveillance on because of the way it was made. Also, because the entire street was a drug-infested area. Everyone on it was either a junky or a dealer. Not to mention the old people who had been living there forever. The GBI received a tip about a Jamaican named Mishna who was actually doing it pretty big right under their noses. However, they couldn't cut the deal with Brian Macklyn yet. They needed something solid on the two names that he'd given them.

The other guy, they already knew about, Juggernot. An older dealer about forty-five or fifty. He'd been around for a while but he wasn't stupid. Juggernot didn't in any way touch anything other than marijuana. Even that wasn't enough to hit him with a federal indictment. Juggernot had workers, and they used some type of complex code that they hadn't been able to break yet. But this guy,

Brian, was telling them both Juggernot and this guy Mishna were all tied into the same Cuban they were after, Carnelito.

"So, let me get this straight," Francis said, looking across the table where Jasmine sat. Looking too good in the *Perry Ellis* form-fitting dress with the *Dolce & Gabbana* platforms on. When she went to change, he had no idea that she was stepping into a phone booth and she was already on fire. "The nigga had money and guns up in your apartment. And you didn't know about it?" he asked.

They were sitting in a restaurant called California Dreams, which was on Washington Road. It was one of those either, or dress code places. Jasmine was actually loving the social atmosphere, right now. She also loved the fact that he'd put on some *Fred Perry* khakis with a nice *Coogi* sweater that went perfectly with the black *Timberlands* which had bubble gum soles. It was nice and thuggish.

"I mean, he never brought his drugs home," she was explaining. "So, I didn't expect the guns either. I wasn't surprised about the money. He did pay seventy-five percent of everything in the apartment. And that was with the drug money he made, so—"

Francis still shook his head. He watched as she picked up her glass and drank some champagne, it was called *Rose*, by *Perrier Jouet*. This was the first time he'd had it, but it was only one on the menu he could pronounce.

"So, you've been home what three months now? And still, there's no girlfriend?" she asked.

They'd been in the restaurant now for an hour. The sun had gone down completely outside, and all they did was drink champagne and talk. They'd eaten earlier, now they were getting to know one another.

"Truthfully," he stated. "I wasn't in a rush to find one. I mean, to be honest, I'm a little too old to be on the boyfriend/girlfriend shit. And I'm really a street nigga for real. I don't have time to be an actor."

"Okay, now that's what I call *real talk*." Jasmine laughed. "There aren't a lot of guys who feel comfortable expressing themselves the way you do. And that's different, so if not a girlfriend, then what *a cut buddy*?"

Francis thought it over, he'd picked up on a lot of the modern terms. Especially while hanging with Young Castro. So, he knew exactly what the term meant.

"I mean, are we being grown? Or are we tossing around words and terms to try and figure out what we're comfortable saying? Or what can and what can't be said?" he asked with a serious expression

Jasmine took a minute to consider the question and what it might imply. "I guess we're both grown. I mean it's not as if I'm sensitive or anything. As long as you're not planning to curse me out or anything," she said.

Francis emptied his glass, then refilled both of them again. He looked directly into this young beautiful woman's eyes and explained his realty. "What I want, is a woman. A woman that belongs to me and that I can trust. Girlfriends are temporary relationships. And I'm at an age where I'm thinking about babies—" He paused to consider his next words. "So, there's definitely a job opening. And you damn sure qualify. However—" He paused again. "—if you still feeling your ex-cool. And if you wanna be friends, I'm cool with that, too. But I think it's only fair that you know. I definitely want to get all up inside your life. I have thought about it since I first saw you in that store, which means if you ever spread your thighs and invite me in, I won't hesitate. And I won't wear a rubber because my intention will be to put my seed inside you."

Jasmine sipped her champagne. She wasn't really surprised by the way he spoke. All her life she'd been watching hood movies, reading hood books, and listening to hood music. So, she knew this was what she had been waiting for. Brian was street, but he wasn't this hood.

***

"I'm so hood. Yeah, I wear my pants below my waist and I never dance when I'm in the place that you and yo' man is planning to hate—"

The first kiss was shared while they were both still standing in the middle of her living room. He took his time, exploring her mouth and the thickness of her lips. He wasn't in a rush, but then she broke the kiss and took his hand. Jasmine kicked off her heels as she led him into her bedroom. Inside the room, Francis was standing behind her as they stood in front of her bed. He placed his arms around her and began kissing her on the neck. She stepped forward, and he watched as she removed the dress in one motion.

He saw that she wasn't wearing a bra and even though, she was as light as she were. Her nipples were like brown strawberries. He watched as she sat on the edge of the bed with her panties still on, and waited while he undressed. Once he'd removed everything, he stood there a moment so she could take in all of him. Jasmine was indeed impressed. For a thirty-nine- year old man he had the body of one those guys in muscle fitness magazines, and he was hung a hell of a lot better than Brian.

She knew they said with age came experience, but he'd been in prison for twenty years. Francis moved forward and guided her back onto the bed. He took a moment to kiss her again, and soon was moving down to her neck. When he reached her nipples he took his time and showed equal respect to them both. Then he continued moving down southward. At her belly button, he took his time and explored it with care and interest. While doing so his hand grasp her panties and she lifted her hips so that he could remove them, all while she still had her legs raised. Francis placed one across each shoulder, then his tongue began to explore her life.

"I'm so hood, and I got these golds off in my mouth. If you come closer to my house, then you know what I'm talkin' 'bout—"

Jasmine had to fight for breath as he caressed her clit. Then he began making small circles around it and every now and then his lips would close on it and he'd suck lightly. She'd only had this done right once and that was with a white guy she'd dated in high school. She'd never thought to meet a black man who really knew what he was doing. Until now, she came twice, back to back and he drank it as if it were nectar.

"Baby, wait." She pulled him up and began kissing and sucking on his lips.

In the process of doing this Francis shifted until his dick was now lying on her stomach. He pushed her legs further apart as she reached down and guided him. Francis was looking down into her eyes as he began to sink deep into her life.

"Oh, God!" she breathed as the lyrics of a certain song ran through her mind.

"I'm out the Hood and if you feel me put yo' hands up. Hood, my hood niggaz gon' and stand up. I'm so Hood and if you not from here you can walk it out, and you not hood if you don't know what I'm talkin' 'bout—"

Francis had to pause because he could feel her muscles as her inner walls contracted and squeezed him on his inward stroke. When he pulled back it seemed like she was trying to hold on to it and not let him take it away. He'd been dead serious about putting a baby inside her. He definitely hadn't bothered with a condom. In truth, she couldn't be mad because he'd told her upfront.

Jasmine was thinking as his body moved inside of hers. That maybe he was the one. All her life she'd had dreams about meeting *that* guy. So, far none of the guys she'd met had been *him*.

Francis began to pick up speed, going just a bit deeper with his thrust. His goal wasn't to beat the pussy up but to finesse the pussy. He was placing his claim on it and letting her know who the boss was from here on out. Jasmine twisted her hips and rode the wave out. They both came together.

"I'm—I'm—I'm, I'm so hood—" the song's lyrics played in Jasmine's mind.

Later

Francis laid there thinking as Jasmine was asleep, he could hear her breathing softly. He wasn't exactly sure where his life was about to go. However, one thing was for certain. If this woman was going to be his woman. Then he was going to do all he could to ensure her happiness.

Jasmine wasn't sleep she was thinking. While Francis laid on his back. She had her head on his chest and she was also feeling some type of way about him at that same moment. She was just hoping he wasn't like all the other guys she'd known. She was praying that he was the one.

Trai'Quan

Chapter Six

"I need your help family," the caller spoke.

There was a small moment's pause.

"Alright, what seems to be the problem?" Noel asked.

He then listened, as the caller explained the problem. That took a while because it was said in code. From what he was receiving, someone went down and were having conversations with the F.B.I. It seemed they were scheduled to testify before a grand jury in Federal Court. Thus, the spoken in code conversation. But all they would have gotten was some talk of a Corvette ZR1 and how it had been beaten by the Porsche 911 Turbo. The Porsche would hit 0 to 60 in 2.8 seconds. The only thing faster was the Bugatti Veyron which reached the 0 -to- 60 mark in 2.7 seconds, but the current owner didn't want to sell.

"Give me a day or two but it won't be cheap," Noel said.

Then the call was ended. There were several ways that he could solve the problem. Noel was thinking. Having the Sandman come all the way from Texas would be real expensive not that *he* had to pay for it. He sat the Galaxy down on the bed next to him. Then picked up the newspaper he'd been reading. They were talking about something President Obama was doing. Since he really liked the guy, most times when he came across stories on him, Noel would read the entire thing. It wasn't until he finished reading the article that he picked the phone back up.

There were two calls that he needed to make. One was to his sister because there were ways for them to communicate that he didn't have to worry about anyone overhearing. Then he made the second call.

***

His cellphone woke him with the DMX ring tone, '*Get at me dogg.*'

Francis sat up and looked over to where Jasmine still slept. It was Sunday, and they'd spent all of Saturday in the bed. He reached for his pants and pulled out his Galaxy. Looking at the screen it read, *Big Dredd.*

"What up, Star?"

"Boy, how ya doing?" Noel asked.

Francis took a moment to outline his situation. He also told the older man about the new woman in his life.

"Good, so you staying outta trouble? You and Mishna doing alright out there?" he asked.

"We ain't been hanging out. I just spent this whole weekend with my Lady. I'm trying to make sure it's solid. But I guess me and him cool. We ain't having bad words. Why is something up?" Francis asked.

"Nah, nah, not that I'm aware of. But I do need you to drive down and see Sheba."

Francis glanced back at Jasmine. He suspected she might be awake, but he wasn't sure.

"Same place as last time?" he asked.

"Yeah, she actually owns that place."

"When you need me to go?" Francis asked.

"Like the next day or so. But how's your thing with the job going?" Noel asked.

"Not too good, I'm thinking about letting it go. Which means I can make that trip later today," he explained.

Lately, he'd been looking into how he could open his own bookstore. There wasn't a lot of money in it, but it would be something he liked to do.

"Is there anything else you need, bruh?"

"You still got some of that gift left?" Noel asked.

Francis laughed, knowing he meant the weed. "Hell yeah, about half actually."

"A'ight, well, just go see the girl. I'll be in touch. One!"

The cell ended, Francis sat there thinking.

"You have to go?" she asked. Having heard all his end to the conversation.

"Yeah, but not right now. The old Dredd needs me to go see somebody for him," he explained.

"How long will you be gone? And what about your job?"

Francis gave it all some thought. Noel hadn't given him any details, however, it sounded urgent. "Probably about a week, but the job wasn't doing it for me anyway. I think I'll try something else when I get back. But hey, don't worry." He leaned over to kiss her. "I am definitely coming back."

"Uh-Huh, you better." Jasmine smiled.

***

Mishna sipped on his Heineken as he sat inside his truck and watched this young nigga Young Castro hustle. Actually, he wasn't hustling at the moment and Mishna hadn't come to 8th and Grand to watch the nigga. Instead, he was parked in the driveway of this bitch name, Tika. A bad bitch who danced at one of the clubs downtown. Mishna was there to give her a ride to work but decided to wait in the truck. In doing so he seemed to see Young Castro and a few of his boys out kicking it. Every so often someone would pull up and buy some weed. But it didn't seem like they were trapping it out.

Either way when Tika came out and got into his truck. He pulled his mind away from Young Castro and drove her to work. He was still wondering what the boy Rabbi was up to though.

***

This time the drive to Buford didn't seem as long as it had the first time. Then Francis thought it may have to do with the fact that he was now familiar with the drive. Having made it once already. Yet, when he pulled up in front of the house and got out. He wasn't surprised to see the Jamaican with the M-4. This time the meeting was peaceful.

"Bum, Star, what up family?" the Jamaican asked.

"Not much, Mon, da Dredd sent me. Is Ms. Sheba expectin' me?" he asked.

"Ya, come," he said.

Francis once again followed him through the house. It seemed just as it was the last time he'd been here. So, he knew what to expect. This time when he stepped out onto the back patio, he found Ms. Sheba standing. Her back was to him, and although she was an older woman, he still took the time to admire her nicely formed ass. When she turned he saw that she held a blunt and was about to light it. The Jamaican who'd led him back there was now gone.

"Ah, de Rabbi. Tell me, are ye religious?" she asked.

"No, not really," he said after thinking about it.

"So, to what God do ye pray?"

He really couldn't answer that, because in prison he'd stop believing in the higher power in the sky.

"I stop praying in prison. I guess when I realized that no one other than me was listening," he said.

Then watched as she used a lighter to put flame to the end of the blunt. Ms. Sheba inhaled the weed smoke deeply. After four good tokes, she held the blunt out to him. Francis took it and did the same. After four tokes he passed it back.

"Der's a man—" she began to speak. "Him in jail, but in a few days, him will be moved to Atlanta. Dis man will go before a grand jury. Once der, him will say tings dat will hurt other people—" She paused to take another hit off the blunt. "Dis man cannot be allowed to speak. Dis Man, for his disloyalty, him need to die," she explained.

Francis thought about it. How exactly was he to kill someone that was in Federal Custody?

As if she read his mind, she said, "Come, I show you how you killed dis man."

He followed behind her, he wasn't sure if it was the weed or not. But he was paying more attention to the sway of her ass. She led him into a room. This room, as he saw held a number of guns. Most were on racks around the room, that was on the walls. There was a long table as well. Ms. Sheba walked over to it, with the blunt in her mouth. She used both hands to lift the rifle and turned to show it to him. Francis was impressed.

"Dis, de TTR-700 tactical sniping rifle. Dis been designed so as de butt can collapse. Der also a bipod and dis scope can see de wings on a fly. De rifle also comes wit' dis silencer. It -grains, make not one sound," she explained. "It shoots federal 168- grains Hpbt bullets. Dis, how you kill dis man." She placed the gun in his hands. Then as she continued smoking the blunt. She watched him look the weapon over and smiled at *the killer.*

***

Lloyd was in the process of going over the following months' court appointments. When his secretary buzzed and said that F.B.I agent Raymond Conklyn wanted to see him. He was vexed by the request.

"Should I ask him to come back, Sir?" she asked.

"No, that's okay Barbra. Send him in," he responded.

He then stood up behind his desk as the office door opened. Senior F.B.I of the CSRA field district, Raymond Conklyn was a pretty big guy. In fact, he was large, as he stepped inside the office he nearly had to bend down to clear the doorway.

"Ray, how are you?" Lloyd reached out as he shook the other man's hand across the desk.

"I'm good Lloyd and you?"

They both seated themselves across from one another. The office door was closed now.

"Fine," Lloyd said, waiting to see what's going to happen with this Chief appointment. "Thus far it looks like I'll get it."

"I hope you do. It'll make some of my jobs a whole lot easier," the F.B.I agent said.

Lloyd laughed. "Yeah, maybe. Only about eight percent of your cases ever see a state court, but tell me. What can I help you with?"

"Well, as you know, this guy Brian is due to appear in federal court next week? He'll be taken to the GBI building on Panthersville Road in Decatur, Ga. He'll be presented in the Decatur courthouse that Tuesday," Agent Conklyn explained.

"Alright. So, how can I help you?" Lloyd asked. He watched as the agent sighed.

"Well, as you know, we cut your daughter loose because there wasn't anything to incriminate her. However, I've been asked to check with her and see if Brian might have mentioned certain things in her presence. Our DA wants to be sure that this guy doesn't wiffle out somehow," he said.

Lloyd gave it some thought. "So, she's not being charged with anything?"

"No, definitely not."

"And what if she overheard something? Will she be drawn into your case?" Lloyd asked.

"No, all we need is the details of what she may have heard. Nothing more. It'll only take five minutes, ten at most," Agent Conklyn said.

Lloyd checked his watch, it was nearly time for lunch. He usually ate with Jasmine any way. This was their family bonding time.

"Tell you what," he began. "We're having lunch together in a few. You're welcome to join us."

"Thanks, Lloyd, I really appreciate it. If you or your girl ever need anything just ask."

As they sat there and continued talking about other things until lunch. Lloyd made it a point to file away the F.B.I agents promise.

***

Francis took I-20 and drove all the way to Atlanta. When he reached the GA perimeter he followed the GPS until he got off on Memorial Drive, near the postal office and corn park. Knowing that today was Friday and he couldn't do the job until Tuesday. He ended up getting a room at the Savannah hotel.

Once inside the room, he placed the large carry case with the rifle in it on the bed. He placed his gym bag with the clothes in it next to it. Then he went into the bathroom and took a shower. Upon finishing his first thought was *food*! So, he called down to room service and ordered something. As he waited he pulled out the park work that Ms. Sheba had given him.

Brian Macklyn, age 29, Black male, 6'1", 192lbs, born in Bronx, New York. There were several photos even a few of him going to the F.B.I.'s office from the jail. Francis then came to a map showing Decatur, GA. The federal courthouse was in Fulton County, but the hearing was at Decatur courthouse. The areas outlined in red were the GBI building that stood between the Georgia Regional Hospital and the Wells Fargo Bank. The other area showed the courthouse. On one side was the Bank of America and further off on the other side was Agnus Scott College.

He couldn't really tell from the map which would be the best place for him to set up. On the map, it looked like they both held potential. He would still need to surveillance both locations in person. That was the only way he would know for certain. There was a knock at the door.

Someone said, *"Room service!"*

***

"Carnelito?" Jasmine said. She sat at the table with her father and F.B.I Agent Conklyn. Who'd been asking questions. "All I've really heard about him was that he was Cuban. I know that he's supposed to be somewhere in Florida and that he has connections to a lot of people," she explained.

Agent Conklyn made notes in his blue notebook. "Have you ever heard the names, Juggernot or Mishna mentioned by Brian? Or any of his associates?" he asked.

Jasmine became thoughtful, mostly because she had heard the name, Misha. By it being a really uncommon name. She didn't think there were two people in Augusta, GA with it, but she hadn't heard the name from Brian or his people. Jasmine knew that Mishna was Francis' partner. The guy she'd first seen him with. She suspected, that for the name to be coming up in an F.B.I investigation, this guy Mishna was a dope boy. Yet, she knew that Francis didn't sell drugs.

'*Maybe, what his friend did while he was in prison, had nothing to do with him,*' she thought.

"No, I've never heard Brian or anyone in his crew mention those two names," she said, which was the truth because she hadn't.

The F.B.I agent asked her a few more questions. Then he told her if she ever needed anything, all she had to do was call him. He'd do whatever he could for her, with that he thanked her, then stood to leave. Jasmine was still deep in her thoughts.

***

"*By the bodega iron under my coat, feelin' braver/do-rag wrappin' my waves up. Pockets full of hope/do not step to me I'm awkward, I box lefty often/ my pops left me an orphan.*" Jay-Z: Renegade

"Yo, where that nigga Poe at?" Young Castro asked.

He'd just pulled up and hopped out of his SUV. There were eight niggas standing out on 8th and Grand. All of them were a part of his crew, both young and the old. Young Castro was the reason they were all eatin' as good as they were. Before he showed up, the other so-called weight men who came through wasn't really showing any love. They had weight, but with their pieces, a nigga couldn't really make nothing.

At the time Raine was going with a nigga name, Point Man. Point Man had the connect, Point Man had been from Southwest Miami. He had his hand into some serious coke, nut Point Man turned out to be a crab. Put fifteen crabs in a bucket with no lid on it and you don't have to worry about one getting out. Each crab would keep one another from crawling out. They'd reach up and grab the leg of one as soon as it looked like he was about to get out of the bucket. They would pull his ass back down.

Point Man would have been the one who put the crabs in the bucket. He created the thirsty/ selfish nigga mentality that evolved on 8th and Grand. He'd only let a select few eat. While other niggas he bird fed. Point Man created a whole lot of jealousy and envy with the way he manipulated the streets. The whole time he was eating *real* good. The crabs were so concerned with pulling one another down, that they didn't pay attention to what Point Man was doing.

Then Raine's baby brother was gun down in a street beefs. A beef that originated with Point Man. Not long after that, the GBI came through three weeks straight. Point Man lost all his crabs. His name was so hot in the streets that he had to leave, and no one knew where he went.

That dry spell lasted nearly a year. Then Young Castro's grandmother Ms. Chrissy passed away. At the time of the funeral Young Castro came down from New York. He was originally born in Augusta. At the Medical College of Georgia. But when his mother fled the South, Young Castro was only three-years-old. So, he was raised in Brooklyn's Brownsville housing. The jungle, where all the citizens were animals. Young Castro grew up famished for the street fame. He just couldn't achieve it the way he wanted in Brooklyn. Poverty being the main reason. He just couldn't get his grip financially. Every hustle seemed to be a poor hustle. It produced no resource that could become productive.

All the bigger Animals who had the said resources weren't sharing. There had been times when Young Castro went hungry. Especially when his moms got turned out on Heroin. He'd been thirteen when the whole situation dawned on him. For five years Young Castro struggled in the streets. His moms passed away from an overdose just before his fifteenth birthday, leaving him alone since he never knew who his father was. Everyone in Brownsville was either Muslim, Five Percenters, or a gangbanger, which was how he'd been raised. Yet, no committing to either one. Young Castro took jewels from each and transformed his life to some degree.

Then he got the word that his grandmother passed away right after his eighteenth birthday. He'd always known his mother's mother. He grew up with the habit of calling her every third Sunday. Something his moms used to do. So, when he called and was told that his grandmother passed almost a week before the call. He had just enough time to make it back to Georgia for the funeral.

Young Castro would have gone back to Brownsville after that. But a lawyer accosted him as the people were leaving the gravesite.

The lawyer explained that he was the only living relative left of his grandmother. Thus, her insurance policy was to be bestowed unto him. Minus funeral and burial cost, he'd also inherited a house. Having never had a house before. Young Castro decided to stay in Georgia. When he received the keys to the house from the lawyer. He also received $32,000, the money left over.

Remembering his upbringing, Young Castro took that money and did three things. One he bought a bus ticket to Pensacola, Florida. Two he bought himself three pairs of blue jeans, six T-Shirts and a pair of all-purpose Timberlands. Using the $30,000 he had left, Young Castro bought three and a half bricks of cocaine, that he managed to get back to Augusta. By the time his twentieth birthday arrived. Young Castro was still under the F.B.I.'s radar because of the way he moved. But he now owned his own detail/carwash. Using the help of the same lawyer to establish it. He controlled the entire 8th and Grand Blvd area.

***

He found Poe trying to romance some new girl that had just moved onto the Boulevard.

"Ayo, Son," he said as he walked up. Then as if he'd just remembered his manners. Young Castro looked at the girl. "Uh, excuse me, Ma. You mind if I have a word wit' yo' boyfriend here?"

The girl herself almost laughed as she saw the look on Poe's face. As if he'd been caught doing something he shouldn't have. She hunched her shoulders and watched as Young Castro led Poe back up the street to where his Escalade SRX was parked.

***

Young Castro wasn't a tyrant, he didn't oppress his three lieutenants, Poe, Dawg, and Cream. Nor did he manipulate the streets the way Raine told him Point Man had done.

"Listen, Pa, you a businessman duke," he began as Dawg and Cream came over. "I know you still got New York on yo' breath, and these country bitches got yo' nose open. But for real God, you ain't got time to be fraternizing with, Jezebels."

"Yeah, yeah. I got you, Son," Poe said.

The problem was when Young Castro blessed his boys with the food for the week. They, in turn, had to bless their dealers. He always made sure there was enough for everybody to eat good, lieutenants, and workers alike.

"A'ight, so tell me. Why this nigga Pete Rose all over by Southside screamin' 'bout he got over on that New York nigga name, Poe?" Young Castro asked.

"What?" Poe asked.

Poe wasn't a small nigga, he was short 5'7, but he had a lot of mass to him, and being from Yonkers he was known for having a rapid-fire temper.

"Yo, Son, I gave that clown a deal because he came through stressing the last set up he got from me was weak. But I ain't lose no fetti. The hook up came out of the grab bag," he explained.

The grab bag was a bag that Young Castro put all the paraphernalia that was leftover after a cook. The grab bag was crumbs and too small of pieces to sell as packages. So, it was used to balance out a street deal with the boosters.

"A'ight, Pa," Young Castro said. "But yo', for the record." He looked at all three of them. "All of our shit is good shit. I don't even squeeze on a cook. I put an ounce of coke in, I get one and a half back. Not three and not four and a half. So, don't be falling for that dumb shit, Pa," he explained.

Then he told them about the five pounds of ganja he'd just gotten from Francis before he left town. He never told anybody where he got the weed. Instead, he was telling them what he was about to hit them with later tonight. Young Castro ran a very lucrative business on 8th and Grand. He wasn't about to see it have any unnecessary problems. Especially if Francis could keep that real smell good coming.

***

Handcuffed and feet shackled, the F.B.I transport officers escorted Brian out of the GBI building. They led him to the van, where one of them stepped in first. The other one helped Brian step up and into the van. Then the one inside connected the chains to the floor mount. Allowing Brian to sit in the seat comfortably.

"That good for you?" the transport officer asked.

"Yeah, it's cool," Brian said.

Brian was outfitted with a bulletproof vest on. Just in case something went wrong. The drive from the GBI headquarters to the courthouse was only supposed to take ten minutes, which was a straight drive. Instead, because the federal DA stressed the importance of this guy's testimony, they would have to drive another route, a safer one. They didn't take Candler Road all the way. Instead, they turned off onto Rainbow Drive, then got onto Columbia. From there they turned onto Highland Road, taking them to Snapfinger Road. They eventually got onto Wesley Chapel Road and found Memorial Drive.

Then they got back onto Candler, turned right by Agnus Scott College, and made another turn by Decatur High School. From there they drove straight to the courthouse. Along the way, neither of the officers saw a tail, and they were trained to spot even the best.

***

Francis was dressed as if he were a custodial worker. He wore the blue janitor's jumpsuit along with the hat. At least that's what he'd worn when he entered the building of Agnus Scott College. He eventually wheeled his janitorial cart all the way to the elevator. Took it to the top floor. Then found the service stairwell. He made it to the roof with no apparent problem. The sun was up, and it was fairly hot. Francis moved over to the edge of the roof.

He looked across the distance. Having already been up on the roof already he knew that he could not only see the entrance, but he could see in through several windows. He opened the bag with the gun in it. He'd been wearing latex gloves since he'd stolen the van he was using. So, he didn't have to worry about prints. He set about putting the gun together. Once he had everything together, Francis turned his hot backward and settled down to look through the scope. He was thirty minutes early, so all he had to do was wait.

***

F.B.I Agent Conklyn met the transport van as it pulled into the courthouse parking lot. He couldn't help but smile. Two of the people that Brian was about to snitch on were under heavy surveillance, Mishna, and the Juggernot. All they were waiting on was for the judge to swear out the warrant. Brian's testimony would get them just that, and he couldn't wait. Agent Conklyn loved it when these pieces of street trash snitched on one another. Because it made the F.B.I.'s job that much easier, with this deal, he hoped one of these guys could give up the whereabouts of Carnelito.

So, what, Brian would walk with Federal probation. It didn't matter, somebody was definitely going down. He was going to be standing there eating ice cream, watching as this son of bitch spilled all his guts. It took them a moment to get Brian out of the van. Agent Conklyn was still smiling as he saw the snitch hobbling across the parking lot.

When they reached where he and his partner stood, he spoke, "How's it going, Brian? You ready for your big moment?"

Brian stopped and looked the two agents up and down. Then he spit on the ground in front of where they stood. "I just remembered why I don't eat pork." Brian screwed his face up. "Because I really hate pigs."

"Oh, yeah. Well, guess what," Conklyn said. "After today you'll be worst than a pig. If word ever gets out to all your Blood homies. They'll kill you for being a *rat*."

"*Fuck you, Pig!*" Brian spat.

"*No, fuck you—R—*"

Before Agent Conklyn could get the rest of the word out of his mouth. Brian's body pitched forward and they saw blood forming at a hole in the back of his head. All the Agents drew their weapons and began looking around, seeing nothing or no one.

***

The federal 168-grain Hpbt bullet was a specially fashioned bullet. It was built on the same concept of the hollow point bullet. When Francis squeezed the trigger sending the bullet across the distance and into his targets cranium, several things happened upon the point of impact. The bullet entered the back of Brian's head in a piercing form, it then condensed and flatten as it penetrated the skull. It doubled in circumference and expanded slightly. Then tore through all the vital brain matter. The point of impact being between the partial lobe and temporal lobe. At the present angle, the bullet didn't stop until it was lodged between the now shredded left frontal lobe and the inner wall of the skull itself.

As soon as Francis saw the body pitch forward, he pushed backward. Away from the edge of the building. He stood, leaving the gun where it was. Then he made an expeditious exit. Ms. Sheba said to leave the weapon because they wanted the statement to be clear. That the assassination was in part because Brian was snitching. That indeed, it was an assassination. They also wanted to give the impression of it being a professional hit. Even if Francis wasn't a trained killer in the same sense of the words. He was nevertheless, quite good at what he did, *killing*.

Chapter Seven

"Suckers/Get your weight up/not your hate up/Jigga man is die-sel/when I lift the eight up/y'all ain't ready to work out with the boy/your flow is brains on drugs/mine is rap on steroids." Jay-Z: Breath Easy

Francis turned the radio off as he pulled the Lincoln MXK into his driveway, then switched the SUV off. He got out and moved around to the back. Opening it he saw the four very large Champion bags. He grabbed the two on top and carried them to the front door, set them down, and returned for the other two. He'd just closed the back of the MKX and reached the front door when Jasmine exited her house. He didn't see her until she was crossing the street. There was nothing he could do about the bags now. He just unlocked and open the door as she reached him.

"So, did you have a nice trip?" she asked.

"I guess you can say that. How have you been?" he asked.

"So, so. Hey, you need some help?"

Before he could say something, she'd already tried to lift the two bags on the ground.

"Whoa, what have you got in these? Bricks." She left one and was able to lift the other.

They entered his house, where he'd set the other two down. Then she set hers down. He went back for the 4th bag.

"Just some equipment I use to workout with while I'm on the road," he explained.

Then noticed the skeptical look she gave the bags. He wasn't worried about her smelling anything. The way the ganja was sealed the smell couldn't escape. The bag she was able to bring in, that one was filled with money.

"But that's neither here nor there." He held his arm up and checked the time. "It's about to be seven p.m. You got anything going on?"

Jasmine lit up. "No, what's on your mind?"

"There's this club I heard about. A Caribbean style club that I wanna check out. Can you be ready by eight-thirty?" he asked.

"Sure, let me just run back to my place and change," she replied.

Francis really wanted to secure the ganja and the money before he left. So, as soon as she went to shower and get dressed. He did just that. Then he called Young Castro and asked if he and Raine would like to join them tonight.

***

Caribbean Sounds was the actual name of the club. It was located on Washington Road. It wasn't real big, only about 20,000 square feet, the atmosphere was dark inside and a large ganja cloud hung in the air. Francis wore a pair of Parasuco pants a Coogi sweater and Vasquez dress shoes. Young Castro rocked Tru Religion jeans with a Maurice Malone shirt and Timberlands. Yet, they weren't even the centerpieces of tonight's performance. At 5'5 Raine was definitely a dark-skinned beauty. She wore a red dress with the crystals in it by Marsey. She was putting on, wearing the Alexandre Birman platforms and a Kenneth Cole watch necklace and earring set.

Jasmine did her one better, she wore the shoulder less black, thigh-length dress by Dolce & Gabbana, with black 2 ½-inch pumps by Reed Krakoff. Her inch-thick necklace with the letter *J* encircled by diamonds was made by Dior her watch by Cartier and her earrings and ankle bracelet were from Kay's jewelers, and she wore a pair of shades designed by Christian Dior.

When she got into the MKX with him, the sophisticated perfume by Boss Jour assaulted his nose and was still lingering. Over and over Francis kept telling himself that this girl was definitely a dime piece.

***

The club consisted of both a live band and a DJ. They got a table near the stage, then Francis and Young Castro went and bought drinks. The women wanted Cîroc while Francis asked for a William Selyem Precious with a lime twist. When Young Castro heard his request he asked for the same. Then they rejoined the ladies at the table. Young Castro pulled out two vanilla flavored blunts and a bag of weed. They watched as he pulled one and passed it to Jasmine. Then he rolled the other and handed it to Raine. As he cleaned his mess up, the ladies lit the blunts.

***

Mishna was watching the news report of the alleged drug dealer that was assassinated outside of the Decatur Courthouse. The reporter was saying that their sources claimed the dealer, one Brian Macklyn had agreed to turn states evidence and help convict several other high profile dealers in Georgia.

"Ain't that some shit?" he said.

"What's that, Thug?" Shoota Boy asked.

He'd just walked back into the room. Yard King left earlier to go check into some of his business.

"This nigga, Brian, was a rat. But somebody plugged his ass before he could give up the goods," Mishna said.

"Pissttt, it's rats all over the streets thug. You'll be more surprised to know even half of them," Shoota Boy told him.

Mishna heard him and discarded it. Shit, the way he saw it, a rat could only tell what he knew. If a nigga keeps his business on the low, he's alright. Then he wondered what Rabbi was up to. He pulled his phone out and keyed his number, it went straight to voicemail.

"Bitch ass, nigga. Probably kickin' it wit' that bitch ass nigga, Young Castro," he mumbled. Then grab the remote and changed the channel.

***

"Boy, you like the ride?" Noel asked.

He'd been on his Facebook page when the call came through but had been waiting on it.

"Yeah, fam, love the ride. I especially like the rims that came with it. They match the paint job," the caller said.

"I know right, I'm just glad I could help," Noel said.

"If my luck holds out, I won't be needing another ride for some time now. But I do know a couple of other people who like nice cars. They might be in the market for something," the caller said.

"Yeahhh, let me get back to you on that. Give me about a month or two. If they still want the services by then. Maybe," Noel said.

Then they ended the call. From the conversation, he gathered there were two other people who had some type of business they needed handled. He would have to see what Francis wanted to do. Truth be told, Noel was trying to help Francis make some money without having to hustle in the streets. Plus, some of these hits were necessary.

***

"Whatever happened to your friend, Mishna?" Jasmine asked.

They'd left the club and were all standing out in the parking lot smoking blunts. Francis had the driver side door of the MKX open, on the CD playing, Roger and Zapp were singing about *Computer Love*. While Young Castro and Raine were doing a slow dance. Jasmine was standing between his legs winding her hips to the music, too.

"What about him?" he asked.

"I mean, I haven't seen him around. I thought you two were tight?" she explained

In his mind, Francis was thinking about some of the flaws he'd begun seeing in Mishna's character. That was the main reason he hadn't told Mishna where he lived now.

"Nah, we alright. He's just got a lot going on, right now," he explained. "We both on different shit that's all."

What he couldn't tell her was that he and Mishna were both living two different lifestyles altogether. That in his line of business he couldn't afford to trust the wrong people. But since she brought him up. He did wonder what Mishna was up to at that moment.

***

Pete Rose wasn't actually the nigga's real name. People just called him that because they said he favored the nigga in the face. More trap stars knew the name better then they knew his government name. He doubted there were five niggas that knew his government. He pulled his Ford Escape into the Citgo gas station at the end of 15ᵗʰ Street, pulling up next to the pumps. Then he hopped out and stuck the gas pump into the tank.

"Goodbye to the game all the spoils, the adrenaline rush/ and you in a drop your so easy to touch/ no two days are alike – except the first and fifteenth pretty much."

He looked up when the Yukon Denali pulled up on the other side of the pumps with the Jay-Z beating. The Denali was the next year's model and it was clean, white and cream with 26-inch Asanti blades fit into some low profile tires.

"And trust is a word you seldom hear from us/ Hustlers we don't sleep we rest one eye up."

Pete Rose began to bob his head and rap along with the music. He loved that Jay -Z shit, too. When his tank filled he replaced the pump and swiped his card.

"And a drought can define a man when the well dries up/ you learn the worth of water without work you thirst till you die/yup."

Pete Rose wasn't even paying attention. He'd turned to walk towards the store when the Denali's back door open and Poe jumped out.

Poe blindsided him with the 4 rings on his left fist. Before Pete Rose knew what happened he'd gone down to the asphalt hard. Then Poe began kicking him to sleep. In the background, Jay-Z's song December 4ᵗʰ played like it was the soundtrack to the ass whipping Poe was putting on Pete Rose. It only lasted a good five minutes in real-time. Poe spit on him and then hopped back into the Denali. Then Cream put it in drive and pulled off. Leaving Pete Rose on the ground bleeding badly and fighting for air to breathe. He wasn't found until the next car pulled up.

***

Her head game was too fire, especially with the cube of ice still in her mouth. Jasmine's mouth slid over him like a glove sliding on to a hand. It seemed to be made to fit. When she added the necessary suction she needed Francis nearly came up off the couch. His left hand slid into her hair as he held her steady. Even though she didn't seem to need any guidance, the damn girl did her thing like a true porn star would.

"If it isn't love. Why do it hurt so bad? Why does she stay on my mind?"

He could barely hear the music as *New Edition* chanted in the background. His toes curled, and the tension in his thighs built up. He had to stop her before he burst. So, he pulled her up. Jasmine, still wearing her dress came up and kissed him. Then she stood between his legs as he sat forward and slid his hands up her thighs, pushing her dress upward as he went. Soon, he was reaching and she removed the dress from over her head. Francis removed the laced black thong that she wore. But left her pumps on along with her jewelry. As he began to sit back and slide his lower body forward on the couch. He pulled her down on top of him. Jasmine straddled him and reached down to insert his erection.

As he slid inside of her, slowly, because she was the one in control of her movements. Jasmine closed her eyes and let her head fall backward. She still couldn't believe that he felt this good. Once she completed her descent, she paused. Allowing her inner walls to adjust to the size of him. Then, as if she were that woman up on the stage in a strip club. Jasmine began to wine and grind her hips to the music.

"Take my money, my house and my car, for one hit of you, you can have it all."

The *Jodeci* song had just started on the CD rotation, which was programmed the way she wanted it. Francis had forgotten about *all* his problems. This young woman now controlled his reality. He looked down to where they were joined and watched the way that she moved. He could have sworn that the girl had been one of those Arabian belly dancers in her past life, but he damn sure wasn't complaining.

***

"So, what are you going to do about your job?" she asked.

They were both lying in her bed. After moving from the living room and gone at it once more. Now they were tired.

"I've got something else on my plate," Francis told her as he thought about it. "That was one of the reasons I wanted to see how a Caribbean club was set up. I'm going to open a Jamaican club. I just have to find the right location for it," he explained.

Jasmine gave it some thought. "But doesn't that take a good deal of money? I mean just to remodel a building will cost," she said.

"Yeah, but luckily, I've got some people who'll loan me the money I need."

"You mean, Mishna," she stated.

He was starting to think she didn't like Mishna for some reason. He just didn't know what it was.

"Nah, Mishna doesn't have the type of money I want to use," he said. "I'll ask Big Dredd to give me a check. That way it'll be a legal loan. I won't have to worry about the IRS or the Feds," he explained.

Jasmine didn't respond, but she was glad he wouldn't be getting the money from Mishna. Because she was sure the Feds were building a case on him. She didn't want Francis pulled into it.

Francis, on the other hand, was forming the plan in his head. He intended to ask Big Dredd to have Ms. Sheba write the check. He would give her the money back out of the fee he'd just been paid for killing Brian. He just needed to cash the check as a business loan, and start his business. Which really wouldn't be too hard. He'd already seen a vacant building he wanted in Southgate Plaza. All he had to do was see about leasing it and remodeling. He could have the club open in a couple of months with enough luck.

'*Yeah,*' he thought as he dozed off. '*I'll text Big Dredd in the morning. So, when he pulls his phone out he'll know what I need help with. But I'ma pull on the people who own that building tomorrow.*'

Chapter Eight

Four Months Later

"If you watch how I move you'll mistake me for a playa or pimp. Been hit wit' a few shells but I don't walk with a limp." 50 Cents: In Da Club

When Mishna saw the call coming from the unknown number, he wasn't sure what to expect. He'd just left Angel's apartment and was on his way to pick up Shoota Boy and Yard King.

"Yo', who dis?" he asked.

Expecting it to be some little bitch he'd forgotten he'd give his number to, but what he heard was another matter altogether.

"Boy, yer a hard one to find," Noel's voice said. "How you been?" he asked.

"Big Dredd, what up, Rude?" he asked.

Having not heard from Big Dredd in nearly six months. At least directly anyway. He was surprised to be hearing his voice now.

"I would have been hit you. But I been busy, and I don't have your number," he explained.

"Yeah, I heard. So, how's that situation looking for you? Is it taken care of?" Noel asked.

The feds had shut down the trap house on Lucky Street. They'd kicked the door in and caught Yard King and Shoota Boy with the guns and some money. It just so happened that Shoota Boy was in the lab at the back of the house when the door caved in. The back door itself was re-enforced steel, so it couldn't have been kicked in. Shoota Boy had enough time to dump all the drugs and stuff into the acid.

They'd charged them with illegal possession of firearms. The money disappeared somehow, but Mishna had been able to get them out. He did know that someone snitched on them. How else did they know about the back door? Then there was the fact that the Feds questioned him when he went to bond Shoota Boy and Yard King out.

"Looks like it is. I had to move my business, though," Mishna said.

"Yeah. So, what's up wit' you and Rabbi?" Big Dredd asked.

Mishna suspected this was the real reason for the call. Because he and Rabbi were on bad terms.

"We ain't speaking, der been some words," he said.

Noel was quiet for a moment. Mishna wondered just how much Rabbi had already told him.

"A'ight, I'ma leave that alone for now. But I really called to put a bug in your ear. You hear me, Star?"

"Yeah, I'm listening."

"There's a kid somewhere near you who runs around playing with dolls. I think the name is, Duck. You know who I'm talking about?" Noel asked.

"Yeah, yeah. I know who," Mishna said.

"That's your problem. The source of all your bad luck begins and ends right there. And I received that from people above the streets," Noel explained.

Mishna knew exactly what and who he meant. There was a booty boy, a *faggot* named Swan that ran with Connie. A few years ago, it had been said that Swan was working for the police, but there was never any proof. Until now, he knew Big Dredd's higher up people were possibly some cops.

"A'ight, Rude. I appreciate the love, bruh," he said.

"Nah, don't mention it," Noel said. "But one thing, though, the thing between you and Rabbi. Y'all need to dead that and soon."

"I hear you, Big Dredd. One!"

They ended the call, Mishna was trying to figure out how this punk knew his business. Then too, he knew Connie knew certain things. Meaning that Connie was the source of information that the punk fed to the police. Yeah, he would have to see about that first chance he got. As for the situation with Rabbi. He'd see him tonight after he picked these niggas up.

***

"Like I was saying, Pa," Young Castro said as he whipped the new Cadillac CTS -V through traffic. He hadn't had it long, only a month. He just had a thing for Cadillacs. The CTS-V was black with chrome rims. "With this new deal, I've got one the table. We might be able to get that business down on Old Savannah Road. Them niggas been asking me if I could fuck wit' em," he explained. Talking about the recent talks he'd been having with Juggernot and his connection. He still hadn't met this Carnelito character yet. But, thus far, from what was discussed, he would be able to buy more weight.

Normally he would have to rent a car and drive to Miami. Then buy his Cocaine and risk the drive back up the Interstate. While he would get good deals that way. He was okay taking more risks. Because the highways were usually hot. DEA was in joint dealings with the State Trooper's Division and wasn't playing. You had to be real good to make it all the way back with cocaine.

As it so happened, Young Castro never rode the main highways back. He took to a lot of side roads and pulled over at motels. The whole trip back would usually take him a week. Due to the way he was raised, patience was a key factor he'd learned. Young Castro was never in a rush. He didn't do anything too fast.

He prided himself on not making those types of mistakes that couldn't be corrected. Some people would fuck up, then try to straighten it up. He preferred to catch the fuck up before it became serious. So, while it took one day to drive to Miami. It would take him six days to get back to Augusta.

"So, here's the thing, Pa." He turned onto another street. Poe was riding in the passenger seat, while Dawg and Cream were in back. They were all dressed nice because they were going to the club.

"I'm gon' need to put one of you, niggas down there on Glass Factory. So, that you can deal with them niggas. But yo' Son—"

He looked at the blunt that he held in his hand. Then placed it in his mouth and pulled out a lighter. He lit it and inhaled the smoke.

"Yo', here's the thing," Young Castro continued, "I'ma be putting the whole cake in that nigga's hand. So, it's gon' be on that nigga to cook the shit and cut it. This shit gon' be like what—" He hit the blunt then continued, "—like, what Frank Lucas put down wit' that blue magic, Pa."

All his Lieutenants were eating good. The way he made it was so that they could never get greedy. They could never claim they weren't making enough money.

"Listen, Pa." He pulled into the parking lot of the Southgate Plaza and found a parking space. "This is a big opportunity, Son. It's like you gon' be the man, and I'ma be yo' connect. So, do you think you can handle that, Pa?"

He waited as Poe thought about it. Young Castro didn't offer them any of the blunt. Because all three of them had their own blunts. They just hadn't hit them yet.

"Yeah, God. I can hold it down," Poe said.

"Good, now come on. Let's go fuck some bitches," Young Castro said.

They all exited the car, then started walking to the front of club Jamaican Funk. There was long line out front. But the doorman looked up and smiled when he saw Young Castro and his crew coming to the front.

"Brother Man, what's real?" the 6'5', three-hundred-pounds bouncer asked as they waited for him to let them in.

"Life is real. How you doing, Pa?"

"Good, bruh. I appreciate you hooking my old lady's ride up, too. One love, bruh," the bouncer said.

"No problem, Pa. Just bring that Range you got through. I'ma really hook that muthafucka up. But yo', Son. This kid got our names on the list?" Young Castro asked.

Not that he had to, he knew Francis had him and his boys name permanently on the guest list. So, when the bouncer checked. For the sake of the others waiting in line. He had to make it look good.

"Yeah, yeah. Come on," he said.

Young Castro led his boys in.

***

Jamaican Funk was 32,000 square feet of space and since it had once been a department store building. It gave Francis a lot to work with. He had three stages, and two dance floors. One of the stages held a DJ booth, the other two were at either end of the club. They were for the live bands or singers who performed. The bar was larger than usual, it took five women to work it. Behind it, Jasmine was the manager. Raine and three of her homegirls worked for her. She still had her job at the jail, but at night she ran the bar.

She was in the process of checking the inventory of the drinks when Young Castro and his crew pulled up. Raine was over on the other side working. So, she didn't see them at first.

"What's up Ma, where wifey?" he asked.

"Over there." Jasmine nodded down the bar where it curved. "What's up?" she asked.

"Lookin' for your man. He around?" he asked.

"He's in VIP, I think he's got company, though."

Even as she said it, she knew Young Castro wouldn't care. If he needed to talk to Francis, he would definitely talk to Francis.

***

"So, Big Dredd said we should kill the beef," Mishna said as he sat across from Francis in the VIP lounge. The room itself was large, in fact, out of the seven the club had. This one was Francis' personal VIP lounge and was more lavish than the others. The walls were lined with mirrors along three sides. The open side looked out into the club. These weren't regular mirrors, they were more like black glass that held reflections. There was a large couch that formed a letter *C* in the middle of the room. A table was placed in the center of it, there were also speakers where the sounds were pumped into the room.

Francis looked across at Mishna. He'd already talk to Big Dredd. So, he knew what the older man said, and respected it. He just wasn't sure Mishna respected it the same way. Mishna, he thought, had some other shit going on. He just couldn't figure out what it was at the moment.

"Yeah, he called me," he said. "And I gave my word that I would be family wit' it. So, we good."

The beef itself came about as a result of Mishna saying some disrespectful things to Francis's face. He'd said that Francis had become soft. That prison must have brought the bitch out of him. Francis had told him that because he was Rasta, he would forget that he lost his manners. What he didn't tell Mishna, was that the very *next* time he said something like that to his face, would be the last day he breathed.

Before Mishna could speak, though. There was a knock at the door and the bouncer Big T stuck his head in.

"Your boy, Young out here," he said.

"Yeah, send him in."

He saw the way Mishna's face twisted as Young Castro entered the lounge, but he caught himself.

"Yo,' what up, Pa?" Young Castro gave him a fist bump. Then head nodded Mishna. He dropped down on the couch next to Francis. "Listen, Pa, I just got a batch of that good. Shit, you and yo' mans' want to get a sample of the shit?" he asked.

Francis had long ago explained to Young Castro that, other then Raine him, his sister and Jasmine. No one knew that he had the ganja. He'd also explained that he really didn't want Mishna to know.

"Yeah, where that shit at?" Francis said.

Young Castro pulled out another vanilla. He sparked it up and passed it around. When he and Mishna had those words, Young Castro had been present. So, he knew there was tension, but he never spoke on it.

Francis knew Mishna was under the impression that Big Dredd gave him the money to start the club. He knew that had a lot to do with his attitude that day. Because Misha had a jealous streak that seemed to consume him. It was almost as if he was unaware of it. That it existed subconsciously inside of him. They'd no sooner finish the blunt when Young Castro pulled an ounce out of his pocket and handed it to Francis. Then excused himself and went back out into the club.

"Damn, I wish I could find out who his plug is," Mishna said. "That's some of the best ganja in the city. And the shit just keeps getting better."

Francis didn't say anything. He could sense Mishna waiting to see if he would reveal Young Castro's source, however, he was far from stupid.

Trai'Quan

Chapter Nine

The hair salon was called Inez' Styles and stood on the side of Southgate Plaza. Down from the restaurant, between the jewelry store and the new gym that hadn't been open long. Her clientele at the business consisted of nearly every drug dealer's girlfriend, wife, sister, or mother in Augusta. Inside, there were six chairs where Inez, Connie, a homosexual name Swan, and three other women did hair. They did any and every type of hairstyle that could be imagined. It was also at Inez' that the daily gossip was spread.

"Gurl, did you hear about that nigga, J-Dogg?" one of the other women getting their hair done asked.

"Well, you know a few months ago. Somebody killed that snitching as nigga, Brian. And J-Dogg was one of his scraps. The one Brian left the dope to!"

"Nah, girl, he didn't leave it to him," another girl put her two-cents in. "J-Dogg knew where the dope was hidden. So, he went and got it. He told everybody that Brian left it to him."

"Well, just the other day, I was out washing my car and these two blood, red Dodge Durango's pulled up. Gurl, they had them new Giovanni 26-inch rims on them. But they had New York plates," she explained.

"Bitch, will you get on wit' the news," Connie said.

"Oh, well, I saw the five niggas jump out and run up on J-Dogg. Talking 'bout this nigga Brian owed money to some niggas in New York. Gurl, they told that nigga he gon' have to pay it."

"Ain't that some shit?"

"I'd be damn if I pay for some shit a snitch owed."

The whole time the gossip went on, Lisa sat there while Swan did her hair. She really could care less about J-Dogg and everything else. On the other hand, Swan was listening. He had a pending possession coming up in court in two weeks. So, he was trying to find something he could give Agent Conklyn to make that go away. So, far he hadn't heard any of the names Agent Conklyn told him he was interested in, but he was damn sure listening.

***

"Gurl, you fixing to leave?" Raine asked as she and Jasmine stepped into the salon for their appointment.

"Hell yeah, I didn't know y'all were coming in. Hi Jasmine, how you doing sis?" Lisa asked.

"Tired girl, these two jobs don't play," Jasmine said.

She gave Lisa a hug, then took a seat. Raine went to check them in.

"So, what's my brother been up to?" Lisa asked.

"He's been all-in with the club. That and getting ready for the baby. We're looking for a house," Jasmine said, she was six weeks pregnant.

"I know right, isn't it about time you let one of your jobs go?" Lisa asked.

"Try both of them," Jasmine told her. "Francis has me training Raine to be a manager. But says I'll have to quit both jobs in the next four weeks."

"Well, at least you get to sit up and live like a dope boy's girl," Raine said as she came back.

"Nah, that's you girl. Francis ain't even rocking like that," Jasmine corrected.

The conversation turned to Young Castro and there was a mention of Mishna. The speculation was that Young Castro was doing business with Juggernot. It was a foregone conclusion that he would bump heads with Mishna. Everybody knew Juggernot and Mishna were competing for control of Sunset.

***

Swan definitely got his ear hustle on. All three of those names were at the top of Agent Conklyn's list. Now all he needed was something juicy and he might not have to see the inside of the court-house after all.

***

"Ayo thug, you still ain't tell me who we out here watching. Is it yo' man's wit the club?" Shoota Boy asked.

While he sat next to Mishna in the rental Infinity Q50. They were inside the Southgate Plaza, and there was so much going on. Shoota Boy must've assumed that since the emerald green Denali XL pulled up that this was what they'd been waiting on. Francis had traded the MXK in and gotten the Denali a little over two months ago. They watched the truck parked in front of the club. Then Francis got out and walked inside. But that wasn't why they were there. Mishna looked at his Bulova which he'd spent ten grand on. He saw that it was almost 6:00 p.m. He wondered how much longer before this booty boy left.

***

"What's going on, Phillip?" Francis asked as he entered the club.

"Everything's good, Mr. Santos. We still opening at the same time right?" Phillip asked.

There were only five people in the club at that time. Phillips and four other bouncers, who were responsible for making sure the security is the way that it should be.

"Yeah, everything will be going according to plan," Francis told the large man.

Then he made his way to the office at the rear of the club. Once there he made him a drink of the Hennessy Black that he kept in the office. Then sat behind the desk. On the desk, there was an Apple computer. He hit a few buttons. Then put in his password. There were only three people other than him who could access the computer. That was Jasmine, Raine, and Phillip. No one else had a reason to be on it. However, Francis had a Myspace site that only he could access. Along with several other pages that Lisa had come in to build for him. It was on one of these that he noticed a message that read: *Go see Sheba in your spare time.*

***

Swan pulled his pink iPhone off his hip and checked the message. It read: *//: Under the 15th Street overpass at 7:30.*

It was about to be 7:00 on the head, so, he finished cleaning his workstation and looked to Inez.

"Ms. Inez," he said in his female imitation voice. "Gurl, I've got an appointment in thirty minutes. Is it okay for me to leave once I've cleaned up?" he asked.

Inez looked around, they were really through for the day. All they were doing was the customers.

"Yeah, you cool. But, hey, have that ass up in here first thing in the morning. We've got a full day tomorrow."

Swan finished what he was doing and snatched up his purse and keys.

***

"Pipe up, thug," Mishna said.

Shoota Boy had dozed off over in the passenger seat. As soon as Mishna spoke, he came up and reached for his Sig-Neuhausan 9mm. He glanced around looking for the target. All he saw was a punk getting into a hot pink Chevrolet Equinox.

"What, where the beef at?" Shoota Boy asked.

Misha nodded to the punk. "The Equinox, but we ain't gon' hit him here. So, just sit tight."

Shoota Boy was confused, but he knew not to ask too many questions. He'd been with Mishna long enough to know that, for whatever reason he wanted somebody dead. It was a good enough reason for him to do it.

***

Jasmine and Raine had stepped out of the salon just when her Galaxy vibrated on her hip. She pulled it off and read the text.

"What's wrong?" Raine asked.

"Francis need me at the club. You gon' have to go without me," she said.

Then she turned and walked across the parking lot to the front of the club. Once there she knocked, and Phillip opened it.

"How you doing, Boss?" he asked.

"What's up, Phillip. Where Francis at?"

Just about all the staff called her boss instead of Francis. As if they really worked for her.

"He's in the office."

She walked that way, speaking to the other guys on the way there. When she reached the office she found Francis sitting at the computer.

"Damn, that was fast, I just text you."

"Me and Raine were over at Inez's getting our hair done. So, what's the problem?" she asked.

"I need to make a trip, I'll be gone for about a week. So, I'll need you to run the club while I'm gone," he explained

"Okay, when?"

"Tonight," he said. "I'll be leaving in about an hour. You cool with this?" he asked.

It had become a habit of sorts over the past four months. He would up and leave to do something for Big Dredd and she wouldn't ask what.

"Yeah, I'm alright," she answered.

Francis looked up at her to be sure. Because some people would say one thing but their body language said something else. At the moment he couldn't tell, though.

***

Agent Conklyn stood beside his unmarked Sedan smoking a cigarette and listening to the homosexual's report. His partner was sitting in the car. The report wasn't as good as the past information he'd received, but he listened anyway. When he was finished Agent Conklyn told him what he needed. The homosexual said he would try and find the information. Completing that task, the homosexual got in his SUV while Agent Conklyn got back in the car, then they parted ways.

***

Swan made a left, then drove down to Augusta Avenue and stopped at the stop sign. He was able to breathe easier now. Knowing that the possession case would be taken care of. Now he had to find a way to get the rest of the information. He made a left and turned on the Augusta Avenue, then continued driving. This was a part of the city he knew good, it was where he usually got his crack. Since he was already down there, he looked for his usual dealer. Swan was driving slow looking when out of the blue a vehicle pulled around and in front of his SUV.

"Hey!" he shouted and blew his horn.

When he saw the young thug exit the vehicle with the gun clutched in his hand. Swan knew his life was at an end.

"Lord Jesus, please welcome me into your kingdom," he prayed.

Shoota Boy stood at the window a second with the 9mm extended and turned sideways. He could hear some of the prayer, but after he realized what the punk was doing. He went ahead and squeezed the trigger. Flame spit from the barrel and the gun jumped in his hand three times. When the punk fell forward with his head on the stirring wheel, blowing the horn in the process. He glanced around and made sure no one saw him. Although, in this area, nobody would talk anyway. He turned and jumped back onto the Q50.

"What's up, any problems?" Mishna asked.

He backed up, then put the SUV in drive and sped off down the street.

"Not really, this fuck nigga was praying to Jesus," Shoota Boy said. He paused as if he were deep in thought. "Ayo, Mishna, let me ask you something, thug."

"What's on your mind, thug?" Mishna asked.

"Ayo, you think fuck niggas go to heaven?"

Mishna thought about the question. "I really don't know, bruh," he said. "They say Jesus died for the sins of man. And since it's a sin to be a fuck nigga in the first place. Maybe they've got a place up there for them to, Star," he explained.

Shoota Boy thought about it some more. Mishna could tell the young gunner was having some serious religious thoughts at the moment. So, he waited, wanting to give the best advice he could. But he himself wasn't a diehard religious person. He believed in the king, Selassie! He believed in Rastafarian. But he'd never really been in Jesus and all of them other guys.

So, as he drove, waiting to hear what Shoota Boy was about to ask him next. Mishna also asked himself if he believed in heaven or hell. Because, he'd always thought that heaven was when you inhaled the ganja so deeply that you weren't sure if you'd exhaled the smoke, and that hell was not being able to get the ganja in order to inhale the smoke.

"Mishna," Shoota Boy said.

"Yeah, what up, thug?"

"Man, if they let fuck niggas through the gates. Man, I don't think I wanna go. They just gon' be fuck niggas up there too," he stated.

"Yeah, I guess you right." Mishna had never thought of it that way.

"How they gon' call it Heaven after they let the sin come in?" he asked.

They were both in thought as Mishna kept driving.

Trai'Quan

Chapter Ten

Francis had driven Jasmine back to her house so that she could get her Porshe Cayenne. He'd traded her GX460 in and brought the champagne, pink Cayenne for her birthday. She watched as the tail-lights of the Denali XL went up the street and turned out of sight. Then she ran inside her condo real fast to change clothes. While doing this, her phone rang.

"Hey, baby, how are you doing?"

"Oh, hi, dad. I'm fine, just have to go to work at this other job early tonight," she said.

"Why is something wrong?" her father asked.

"No, Francis was suddenly called away on business. And he asked me to open and close while he's away."

" Don't you think that's a lot of stress for someone in your present condition?" he asked.

Now she was snatching up her keys and on her way out the door. Her father and mother knew that she was pregnant and couldn't wait. They also loved Francis, especially since he made it a point to ask her father for help with the legalizing of the club. He'd needed an alcohol license and her father had helped.

"By the way, I have been meaning to talk to you about that," Jasmine stated. "Francis says he wants me to stop working altogether in a few weeks."

"Well, that sounds about reasonable of him. I'm in agreement with that."

She got into the Cayenne and started it. Then she backed out of her driveway.

"And I'll be looking for a house for us," she said.

"Well, there are some nice houses out our way. Maybe your mother could help you find a good one," he said.

Her parents lived out near Quail Hollow, a nice area, but Jasmine wasn't sure she wanted to be that close to them. She was thinking maybe Wood Lake or Pepper Ridge.

"I'll give her a call, right now, I have to get back to the club. Love you." She ended the call.

A deeper part of her conscious mind wanted to know exactly what Francis did for Big Dredd. She knew about the weed he would bring back. In a way, it made some sense. If Big Dredd was giving him the weed, he'd gone to prison as a result of something he did for Big Dredd. There was just something that kept telling her it was more than that. Then there was the gun collection he had.

She didn't know why he had seven different guns, but he did spend time at the shooting range on Fort Gordon with a guy he met named, Rush. She also suspected Rush was the one selling him the guns. But he and Young Castro would go out to Fort Gordon to shoot twice a month on Saturdays.

Yet, other than the marijuana she knew he wasn't in the streets. Young Castro was the one who sold that. In fact, he was the one who hustled. All Francis did was focus on the club and the book he was writing on the computer, called: *A Heart In Augusta*. He said it was about a Hitman who fell in love. However, she hadn't even read it yet. He said he was nearly finished, and she could read it then. Jasmine pulled into the plaza in Francis's personal parking space, then got out.

***

"Nah, nah nigga. No dice, let me get them, Pa," Young Castro said.

"What?" Easy looked up at him stupidly. "Nigga that throw was clean. Brakes tell him that was a clean throw, thug. I seen it."

Young Castro stood there with his money clutched in his left hand. He glanced around at everybody present. They were in the back of A.C. Greg, which used to be the alternative school. There were a basketball court and a path that went through an opened fence going into Kent Circle apartments. At this dice game were all dope boys. Lil' Henry from Kent Circle, with his partner Dap. The nigga Ace from D.S. along with a few of his boys. Juggernot and his right-hand man Pipe. Both of them were from Sunset. Easy Money and Good Brakes were from Southside. There were a few others out there but everyone present had money.

Young Castro looked at the duo, the throw wasn't clean. He'd watched the nigga slide the dice, which is illegal and a justifiable call in the hood.

"You know what, Pa," he said. "If I was a broke nigga, Son. I would probably ask you to shoot the grown man with me for that one." He looked from Easy to Brakes. "You and yo' mans', Pa."

Easy Money looked sideways to where Ace stood. Ace threw both his hands up like he had nothing to do with it. The whole game it seemed like Easy and Young Castro were destined to bump heads.

"Wait a minute," Easy Money said. "Did this nigga just give me an invitation to that ass?"

He looked at Brakes, who was nodding his head. Both of them were not small men. Good Brakes stood at 6'5 and every bit of three-hundred, ten pounds, but he had a spare tire in the waist. Easy Money was 6'3 and two-hundred, eighty-five pounds, he also looked like he hadn't exercised since he came home from prison.

"Come on, man, let's get the next bet down," Ace said trying to kill the beef. "Bruh said he ain't trippin' it."

"Nahhh." Easy Money stood up. He looked over to where Young Castro was standing. "The nigga said, he would shoot the one. Is that what you saying, nigga?"

By now everyone knew the dice game was over. So, they started stuffing their money in their pockets and moving back out of the way. When the circle formed, there was only Easy Money, Good Brakes, and Young Castro standing in it. At 6'0 and his current weight two-hundred, five pounds, Young Castro had been spending quite a bit of time training with Francis lately. Thus, he was far from intimidated by the two larger men. Instead, he sized them both up. He remembered something Francis told him. That any real fight only lasted a good minute and a half. In the first sixty seconds, a serious fighter could end it before it even started.

Young Castro had come to the dice game dressed to swing by the club later. He was wearing Enyce jeans an Avirex 2-XL Shirt and dark Timberlands with the bubble gum soles.

"Y'all sure y'all wanna do this, Pa?" he asked

"What, nigga!" Easy Money started removing his jewelry, that was his mistake.

* * *

Young Castro didn't even hesitate. He moved so fast that he wasn't even sure Easy Money knew it was on. While still clutching his money in his hands. He threw a left, right jab that caught Good Brakes by surprise. The punches came so fast, he couldn't retaliate. The two jabs were followed by a strong left hook and a Mike Tyson uppercut, with the elbow. Good Brakes was out cold before he hit the asphalt. When he turned, Young Castro saw the fear in Easy Money's eyes. He hadn't even removed his watch as he saw his partner removed.

"Whoa, whoa! Hold up, thug," he said.

Young Castro was already focused. He'd already punched the stopwatch, starting at sixty seconds. He twisted his whole body backward and connected a backward elbow to the side of Easy Money's head. Then he dropped low and shot a left hook to his kidney that made his body flinch. He wasn't sure, but he also thought Easy Money pissed on himself.

When he bent forward Young Castro grabbed the back of his head and shot him a knee that broke his nose. Everyone watched as Easy Money and Good Brakes laid on the ground. While Young Castro checked his clothes and money to make sure they weren't bloody.

"Next time I call them dice, Pa, respect my call," he said, not sounding aggressive.

Then he held his arm up, looked at his $2,000 Hublot, and saw that it was almost 8:00.

"Ayo' Son," he called out to Juggernot. "I'm about to go to the Funk. Find me some bitches to fuck and pull up on me tomorrow, Pa."

He turned and walked to the parking lot where his new Mercedes Benz SL-class convertible was parked. The car cost him

$132,000, which he'd dropped just last month. He'd gotten Raine the Mercedes Benz M-class, she was loving it.

***

"Dis man, him in Louisville, Kentucky," Ms. Sheba explained as she stood in the room with the guns. Francis stood next to her. Looking at the pictures of the old white man. It showed him entering a bank. "Him own dis bank. But him crooked and do bad business. Dis man, he have to die," she said.

Along with the picture, there was other information. Francis saw that someone outlined all this guy's activities and daily functions.

"Should it be done a certain way?" he asked, watching as she spread her arms to indicate all the guns that were in the room.

"Dead is dead. Der lots of weapons here. You choose," she told him.

Francis wasn't sure yet. So, he didn't know exactly what to pick. He decided to study the information first and see what was in it then he would know.

***

Noel was pissed and that was a problem. Because he usually had better control of his emotions. He hardly ever got mad, let alone pissed. He opened his locker and pulled out the jar of Folgers. He opened it and used the spoon to put a few scoops in his cup. Then he closed it and walked out of his room. Before he made it to the microwave someone stopped him.

"Say, Big Dredd, you have a chance to look into that business I talk to you about?"

The guy was a portly fat guy who stood 5'8 and well over three-hundred pounds. His name was Charles Keith, he was in for fraudulent activities.

"Not yet, Charlie. It is at the top of my list," Noel said.

Charles bowed his head and said thanks. He wanted Noel to see if his people would be interested in some of the stock markets he'd been into. Noel was still thinking it over. He understood the whole concept. But wasn't sure if he wanted to take the risk. He put water in his cup, then placed it in the microwave.

The female C.O. waved at him and he returned the greeting. Remembering that he had to look into insurance work for her this weekend. The timer rang, he got his coffee and started back to his room. Once there he pulled his phone out and checked his messages. Good, Rabbi had received his instructions and left. That was the message from his sister Sheba.

He still couldn't believe this crazy-ass Jew had the nerve to steal 1.6 million from him. Then continue living his life like nothing would be done about it. As soon as he found out the banker was playing skim games with his money. He transferred what was left to another bank. Most of his money was in banks overseas. But there were a few shell corporations that he ran here in the states. These businesses consisted of several million per company.

While the 1.6 million didn't hurt him to the point he couldn't get it back. It was more the principle. The fact that the Jew *thought* he was untouchable, he was about to find out that wasn't reality.

Chapter Eleven

Mishna didn't see any mention of the homosexual's death on T.V. Why, he couldn't say, maybe it was because he missed a segment. That was the last thing on his mind. At the moment he was headed to the Holiday Inn to spend some time with Inez. That was the one thing he had to give Juggernot. He had himself a bad bitch. The only problem was, Inez was a hoe before she became a made bitch. She'd always had the heart of a hoe and always would. Why Juggernot thought the bitch was being faithful to him, he didn't know. But Mishna was not the type of nigga to turn down free pussy.

The only bitch he wanted to fuck, was the bitch he couldn't, Jasmine. He thought if only he could get that bitch to give him some time. Just once, that's all it would take. Yet, the bitch been acting like her pussy don't stink ever since that rat ass nigga Brian brought her punk ass around the hood. Now, this nigga Rabbi fucking the bitch. Acting like he got himself something with the high yellow hoe. It didn't matter, she was number one on his creep list. Number two was that bitch Raine.

Yeah, fuck that nigga Young Castro. The very first time he caught that hoe on the one. He was definitely going to make a play.

***

William Rossenburg Sr. sat inside of Denny's having his morning coffee, which was a pretty normal thing. Seeing as his wife didn't get up before 11:00 on any day. They didn't hire a housekeeper to live in because neither liked the idea of a stranger being in their home. All three of their kids were grown, and he didn't like the taste of his own coffee. So, he made Denny's the usual stop. This was also a blessing because he was able to get a newspaper, eat a bagel, and sip two cups of coffee in peace.

Other than the professionally dressed black man who he started noticing over the past days. There might have been six other people in there this early. A couple of those were truckers, one was a cop, and others were just people. The black guy drew his attention because they also got their paper from the same newsstand. So, he knew the man was reading the same paper as him. The New York Times, the stock exchange. The way he wore his suit suggested that he too was a businessman. Maybe not as rich as William Rosenburg Sr., who owned his own bank.

***

Francis was aware of the jew glancing his way from time to time. Probably trying to figure out what type of business he was into. Because he'd made it a point to fit in with the business crowd. The suits he wore were expensive. In fact, they were tailored, and all named brand, double-breasted, and comfortable. Either Tricots St. Raphael, Fred Perry, Saks or Dolce & Gabbana. He wanted the jew to see him in a professional light.

Francis didn't ask questions when he was giving these jobs, it wasn't his place to ask. He trusted Big Dredd. So, if he sent him at these people, he knew it was for a reason. Plus, it kept him from having to live the street life. When Jasmine first explained that her old man was the current Chief District Attorney. At first, he nearly panicked, then he met him and found out that Lloyd was actually a good guy. He'd eased his fears a lot. Thus when Francis went to him for some business assistance. It opened a bigger door because he had to explain his past prison experience. By it being a Manslaughter/Assault. He was able to explain it as if he were defending himself. If checked, he would see that Francis had made the claim in court that he was defending himself. South Carolina didn't have a self-defense law at that time.

Lloyd understood and helped him get his club open. Now he and Jasmine were expecting their first child. The club was doing real good, and he was still able to supply Young Castro with the good ganja. So, he wasn't in a position where he had to be in the street. Thanks to Big Dredd. So when he got these calls, he didn't hesitate. That was mostly because he'd come to realize that he had a passion for the killing as well.

Francis folded his newspaper as he saw the police officer finish his breakfast, pay, then leave. While he drank the rest of his coffee. He saw the Jew get up and take his newspaper to the restroom with him.

***

William took the time to clean the toilet, then pad it with tissue before he dropped his pants and sat down. Then it seemed like he let everything out that went in over the past two days. He continued to read the newspaper while sitting there. He'd just turned the page when he heard the door open and someone entered. They walked over to the urinals. Took their time, then moved over to the sink and washed their hands. After that, the strangest thing happened. William heard the person approach the stall that he was in and stopped right outside the stall. When he looked down, he could see the expensive wingtip shoes. He knew that the person was the black man.

William all of a sudden started to become homophobic. He knew how a lot of black men seem to have a craving for the flesh of other men. But then he heard a click and saw that there was now a hole in the stall's door where the lock was. Then the door was pushed in. William looked up and saw the well dressed, black man pointing a small handgun at him, the barrel was unusually long. He registered the fact that it was a silencer at the same time the man pulled the trigger.

***

Francis was kind of surprised that he didn't beg or scream. Either way, after the 4 shots he left the Jew sitting on the toilet with the newspaper in his hand. Then he pulled the door closed and walked over to the trash can. He dropped the .22 along with the silencer into the trash can. He'd kept the latex gloves on until after he'd left.

***

Noel had been sitting at the table in the dayroom working on some law work with another guy. Then his phone vibrated in his pocket. "Give me a sec," he said as he stood.

He walked up to his room and pulled his door up behind him. Then he pulled his phone out and checked the text message. After reading it, he knew the Jew was dead, even though, the message was in code. He texted back and told Sheba what to do next. Then he put his phone back in his pocket, went back out and got back to his law work.

***

"I know I'm trippin', but tell me something." Mishna looked up as Inez came out of the bathroom. She was in the process of getting dressed.

"What?" she asked pushing her earrings back in.

"You're not worried this nigga gon' find out you're fuckin' around on him?' he asked.

"Sounds like you're getting scared?" she said.

"Pisttt, nah, I'm not worried about the nigga. He can't do shit to me," he stated. "I'm just wondering if *you* ain't worried?"

"Child please." Inez slid back on her shoes. "Inez got that good pussy, and you know it. That nigga might suspect something. But he ain't gon' say nothing about it. You think he wanna lose complete access to all of this?"

Mishna looked from where he'd been lying on the bed. She was definitely a bad bitch. Standing there in a dark, pink Seven 4 all mankind jean dress, with three-inch Minola Blahnik pumps on. Looking like she'd just left a photo shoot for King Magazine. Nah, he didn't think the nigga would want to lose all that. Especially since he was the one to make her a bad bitch.

***

Pipes sat in his SRT HellCat Challenger Coupe smoking an apple-flavored black and mild while listening to *Juvenile's 400 Degrees CD*. He'd been sitting there for the past hour. He looked up and saw Inez exit the building, heading to her BMW 6 Series-convertible grand coupe. He shook his head, knowing she was a stupid bitch. She didn't even realize that Juggernot already knew she was slipping. In fact, he'd known months ago. The only reason he hadn't brought it up, was because he was waiting on his lawyer to get the papers ready. Two months ago Juggernot had a private investigator follow Inez for a whole month. Some white dude, he was good. The dude even got pictures of her in the bed with this clown, Mishna.

He watched her pull off, then he watched Mishna come out and get into his new Escalade ESV. Pipes had already taken pictures of them with his phone earlier and sent the shots to Juggernot. He really was just watching now to see how long they would be. Starting his car, he left, too. These muthafuckas had to be as stupid as those niggas who'd tried Young Castro that night, and those niggas were stupid. Pipes still couldn't believe how fast that young nigga moved and took both of them. He shook his head.

***

"Big Dredd, him said give you dis," Ms. Sheba explained. Giving him a bank card for a SunTrust bank in Charleston South Carolina. On the back of the card, there was a name. She'd only given him two of the gym bags of ganja this time.

As he pulled up in front of the large bank. Francis still couldn't understand why Big Dredd would send him to a bank. Granted, he'd asked for the check that one time because he wanted his club to be legal. He parked the Denali and got out. Carrying the card he made his way into the bank. He glanced around until he saw a woman who wasn't busy at her desk.

So, he walked over. "Ahem, excuse me Ms. but do you know how I can find a Mr. Fred Brant?" he asked and watched as the woman smiled.

"Actually it's, Fredricka Brant, she's our manager. One moment."

He watched the woman reach for her phone and make a call. Then she asked his name.

'Francis R. Santos," he said. Then she completed the conversation.

"Take those elevators up to the ninth floor. Her secretary will be waiting for you," she said.

Francis thanked her, then walked over to get on the elevator. He still couldn't understand what Big Dredd had going on, but he went along with it. On the 9th floor a small, thin, white woman met him. She said her name but it was too funny to pronounce. He instead bobbed his head and followed. The secretary led him to an office where she tapped on the door and stuck her head inside. Then she pushed it open to let him in.

Behind the mahogany wood desk sat an older white woman. She looked to be in her 50s, but when she stood, he could see she took care of herself. She was nice, real nice.

"Good evening, Mr. Santos. I'm Fredricka Brant, it's nice to finally meet you." She stuck her hand out.

He shook it as he stepped up to the desk. The secretary had left. So, it was just them.

"Uh, it's nice to meet you, too," he stuttered. "However, I'm not exactly sure why I'm here?"

"Please have a seat," Mrs. Brant said.

After they both sat, she lifted a manila envelope and opened it. "You'll have to answer a few security questions for me. I need to verify you are indeed the right person. Then I'll explain why you're here," she said.

She proceeded to ask him questions. His mother's name, his sister, and his nieces' names. The name of his grandfather, who he almost didn't know. What hospital he'd been born at, etc. He answered all the questions.

Then she looked across the desk at him. "I regret to inform you that your father's brother passed away a month ago. You may not have known him. However, it was to you that he left his small

116

fortune." She gathered her papers. " I'll need you to sign these. And I'll need all five fingerprints of your right hand."

She pulled out a fingerprint kit.

"Why the prints?" he asked.

"Because with an amount of money this size. We'll need to always be sure the right person has control of it," she explained. Then came from behind the desk and fingerprinted him.

Francis didn't complain. "Uhhh, just how much money are we talking about?" he asked.

"Well, it's kind of hard to say." Mrs. Brant returned to her side of the desk. "Your uncle owned a saltwater fishing company, estimated to be about five million. That doesn't include the boats. There are two bank accounts actually. One here, the other is a bank in St. Thomas," she told him. "We hold only one-point-three million of your uncle's money. We don't know the extent of the bank in St. Thomas."

Francis heard all this, but as soon as she'd told him he had an uncle die. He knew this was one of Big Dredd's private businesses. Because his father had been an only child. So, he suspected Big Dredd was giving him a blessing and he wasn't about to argue about it.

Trai'Quan

Chapter Twelve

"Get the fuck outta here, Pa. Ayo, you serious, Son?" Young Castro said.

At the moment, he, Francis, Jasmine, and Raine were all sitting inside the VIP lounge at the club. Francis had only been back for two weeks. In that time, he'd spoken with Big Dredd and gotten an understanding about the company. It was a saltwater fishing company, it was for charter. There were ten boats and at the moment he had people running it. He'd just given ownership over to Francis.

"Yeah," Francis said. "Next week, the four of us will be taking a vacation. I need to go down to St. Thomas anyway and see what business looks like. Unless you and Raine don't want to come."

"Boy!" Raine rolled her eyes. "Quit playing, you know damn well we going."

"Yo, I'm just saying, Pa," Young Castro said. "So, you really a rich nigga now."

He didn't exactly know about rich. The way Francis thought about money. You weren't really rich until you were happy. He looked over at Jasmine, drinking her virgin mixed drink. She couldn't drink alcohol. He was happy with her and the baby they were about to have.

Jasmine had also been happy when he gave her the news. When he'd had to leave that fast without telling her why. She didn't know what to think, but this news seemed to explain a lot. Not that she was glad somebody died and left him a lot of money. She was glad to know that it wasn't something that could put him back in prison. That had been her greatest fear.

Francis also suspected that Big Dredd gave him the business for other reasons. Such as his unexplained absence! As he found out, it was through these boats that the ganja was brought from the Caribbean. He would be receiving far more then what he'd been getting. So, he decided to have a serious talk with Young Castro. Because he would need him to not only step his hustle up. But to secure a place to hide larger amounts of the weed.

***

"Nigga, I know you ain't still mad about that dice game?" Jeeta said as he sat on the hood of his 65 Impala. That had the 3,000-paint job leaving it royal blue which was good with him being a Crip. The Impala also had gold wire Daytons' and 16 switches.

"Don't play wit me, Jeeta," Easy Money stated.

They were all either sitting on their rides, standing next to them, or sitting in them. Present was at least fifteen drug dealers or more, they were outside in the Southgate Plaza parking lot.

"What?" Jeeta asked. "Oh, so now you gon' get mad at the world? Nigga swallow that shit. What's done is done, a smart nigga would go on about his business," Jeeta explained.

He was really getting tired of hearing Easy Money bring the shit back up. Easy Money wasn't a Crip, he just bought weight from Jeeta.

"I don't know if I can let that shit go," Easy said.

A few girls walked by, looking like strippers. So, they paused to look at their asses.

"A'ight. So, what the fuck you want me to do? I ain't got no beef with the young nigga," Jeeta said.

In fact, what he didn't tell Easy Money, was that Young Castro was *his* weight man. Every time he got five bricks or better from the young nigga he got a sweet deal. Then on top of that, the young nigga was selling him this good bud that he was flooding the city with.

"You still got the hook up on them guns?" Easy asked. "Cause all I need is to get something nice."

Jeeta looked across the space at the man. Having just realized this fool really was stupid. He hadn't been at the dice game that night. But he'd heard the details and from what he heard Young Castro was in the right.

"Look, Thug," He began. "I'm not about to get tied up in this bullshit. I told you, let the shit go. But if you stupid, I might have to find somebody else to replace you," he said.

What Jeeta wasn't saying was, the white guy Rush who he got the guns from, also kicked it with Young Castro and the Jamaican nigga who owned the club. It wouldn't do for this idiot to get loose lip and say his name. Then it might as well be his beef.

***

The two F.B.I agents were also sitting out in the parking lot. Inside of the black Infiniti QX56 that was black with tinted windows. They were taking pictures, in most of them, they got Jeeta, who they also had a file on. Easy Money, he wasn't really a big fish. Their main target was also in the parking lot. Mishna was with his two lieutenants.

"You think the intel we just received was good?" the one with the camera asked.

"Maybe," the other one said.

Their informant had told them that Mishna and Juggernot were both waiting to receive a major drop over the next three to five days. That was surprising, seeing as they'd never seen either of them together. So, to find out that they were both getting their drugs from Carnelito and at the same time. This could be the break they needed.

***

Mishna smoked the blunt as he listened to the music coming out of his system. He was having thoughts of opening his own club. When Rabbi first came home he'd thought, Big Dredd was chomping him off. That the older man wasn't gon' make righteous on Rabbi going to prison by his call. After all, Big Dredd had uncounted millions. Unlike Rabbi, Mishna had still been in the streets. He'd witness Big Dredd's heaven. Had been to the small island off South Carolina's coast. The one that Noel once owned.

An Island, Mishna knew if a muthafucka owned his own island then he had some serious money. He remembered how Big Dredd never drove his own ride. There was always a driver and the many cars he had. The SLS AMG GT Coupe Convertible cost $240,000.

The 918 Spider Convertible Porsche cost $800,000, The Ferrari F12 Berlinetta Coupe cost $350,000. Those were just his get around cars, Big Dredd had at least twenty of them.

He had a mansion on the island, some say it was built brick by brick especially for Big Dredd. He didn't know for sure, but he'd been inside it. The mansion had to have cost twelve million. All of this, he didn't think Rabbi knew. When the Feds came to get Noel. All they took was what they saw. Mishna, like everybody else, knew that Noel had far more than that. He imagined they wouldn't be able to touch that which wasn't on American soil.

After Big Dredd went to the Feds Mishna began to hear the rumors. They said Big Dredd had land in Barcelona, Cartagena, and Bonaire. There were so many rumors that Mishna didn't know what to believe. The one thing he did conclude, was that Big Dredd was a rich nigga. Also, there were still things he ran from the inside. So, before he gave Rabbi the club, he thought the old man was on the bullshit.

Mishna pushed the thoughts aside. He then focused on the upcoming meeting. He was supposed to be getting twenty-five bricks for the low. This was why he was thinking about all the extra money he would make. Mishna was thinking that he could start his own club. All he had to do was find the right location. Then his phone rang.

***

Harrison Jordan a.k.a. Juggernot was also having money thoughts at that very same moment. He'd been trying for the past six and a half months to get Carnelito to sell him more than ten bricks he'd been receiving. Explaining that he'd built a clientele within two other areas. Thomas and Martinez, where he had some white boys who said they could buy six keys or better. At the moment, he was only selling them two and a half to three, he didn't want to lose that business. When they last spoke to Carnelito he told him he could buy twenty at any moment. The Cuban insisted that he had a large load. That there were more people he had to supply.

He was in the process of doing something bigger. Now it seemed that something bigger was there, Juggernot thought. He was upfront. Carnelito said he would wait on the rest. He wanted to get all his people on the same page so that no one would be hurting. Juggernot was thinking about that, and about getting rid of this bitch Inez. He'd married the bitch only because she'd gotten pregnant. When his son was born, he hadn't thought much about it.

She'd been a good bitch then, he would have sworn to it. She'd also been a broke bitch, with nothing going for herself but her sex game. Inez hadn't even had the body she had now back then. She didn't become that fine until after she gave birth to his second son. Her hips and ass went from a size thirty-six to a forty-two, with a small waist. Since she was tall, it all fit perfectly, Inez stood at 6'0.

Before Juggernot thought, she was nothing. After she had his daughter, she had her tubes tied. Now his oldest son Marcus was in college, with his youngest son about to follow. His daughter was still in middle school. Either way, all his kids were old enough now that a divorce wouldn't hurt them. He was going to let her keep the house, her two cars, and her hair salon. He was even going to continue taking care of his kids, but he wasn't going to be her pocketbook.

The bitch wanted to fuck this Jamaican nigga, cool. He wasn't going to stand in the way. As soon as this lawyer got all the paperwork in order. He wouldn't have to worry about the bitch anymore. Just as he thought this, his cell phone rang.

Trai'Quan

Chapter Thirteen

It took place in Burke County out on one of those long country dirt roads. Where the houses were miles apart and when it rained the dirt turned to red mud and became soggy and soft. Making it nearly impossible to drive through. The road itself was so hard to find that only by it being registered on the map system was Mishna able to find it by GPS. He glanced over to where Shoota Boy sat holding Uzi 9mm. Looking up into the rearview he saw Yard King with the SK. He wasn't taking any chances.

There was a lot at stake tonight. He'd be damned if he was getting robbed by anybody. He turned another curve and came into view of the Range Rover Sport with the Lexani rims that he recognized as Juggernot's truck. It was parked on one side of the road and across from it on the other side was a Porsche 911 Turbo. In his headlights, Mishna saw both Juggernot and his partner Pipe standing next to the Range Rover. While leaning back onto the door of the Porsche was a South American. He pulled the Escalade up and parked right behind the Range Rover.

"Yo, don't nobody do nothing stupid. This is grown man business," Mishna said.

Then he opened his door to get out, both of his boys followed with their guns out. The moon being full tonight gave them enough light to see one another.

Juggernot smiled as he smoked a Newport, on the side of him Pipe simply stood in silence.

"I see you got your soldiers on standby, huh?" he said in a mocking sense.

"I'm good, I see Pipe over there. I bet he's got two or three guns on him," Mishna said.

They smiled at one another, neither trusting the other in any way.

"Gentlemen, if you don't mind," the South American said.

Due to the fact that neither one of them had actually met Carnelito face to face, Mishna wasn't sure now.

"You're Carnelito?" he asked

This guy was younger than what he thought Carnelito would be. This guy was about thirty-years-old.

"No, I'm merely an associate of Mr. Carnelito. I thought you both were aware of how these things went?" he said. "I'm here to facilitate a business transaction. And it really doesn't matter who does what. As long as your ends are in order," the man explained. He looked at both groups of men. "You've brought your money I'm sure?" he said.

Pipe turned, opened the back door of the Range Rover, and reached in to pull out an XL gym bag. Mishna stepped back to the Escalade and opened the back door. He reached in and pulled out a large army-style green duffle bag.

"Good, and once you've shown me the money. I'll make a call," he said.

Mishna was looking confused. "Wait a minute. When do we get the dope?" he asked.

Usually when he met to buy his product. He would receive it at the same time he handed his money over.

"Don't worry, Mr. Mishna," the man said. "When I make the call, another car will pull up. That car is further up the road. The people in it are waiting. Trust me, you will leave here with the twenty-five Kilos you're buying."

Mishna and Juggernot watched as the man moved to check each bag. He opened them and siffed through the money. Seeing that all the bills were in fact bills and not shredded paper. He spent about two minutes with each bag. Then stood straight.

"Alright gentlemen, one moment." He pulled out an iPhone and pressed a button. "We're good."

That was all he said, then they waited. The bags of money set on the ground between them. About three minutes went by in silence. Then they saw headlights bend the curb. A Lexus LX570 pulled up and stopped right in front of the bags of money. Behind it, another LX570 pulled up. From the back of the SUV, four men with M-16s stepped out and walked up to the money.

They lifted the bags, ignoring the young gunmen who stood with their guns on display. Once they had the bags of money loaded into the back LX570, the doors on the first one opened and two guys jumped out. The back hatch opened as they went around back. They reached in to grasp two large duffle bags. Each man brought one and placed it in front of Juggernot and Mishna.

"Gentlemen, would you like to check your purchase?" the South American asked.

At that moment, the four from the back of the SUV and the two from the front, all turned towards Juggernot, Pipe, Mishna, Shoota, and Yard King, then shouted. "DEA! Get down on the ground! Get down!"

"No! Fuck," Mishna cried.

As soon as he did, Shoota Boy and Yard King open fire on the DEA agents. Being trained killers, they separated. Causing the agents to focus on two targets. Then Pipe pulled his gun out. The shootout only lasted a few seconds. The DEA agents had body armor on and better guns. In the end, Yard King and Shoota Boy were gunned down, Pipe was also killed. They had Juggernot and Mishna face down in the dirt road.

Then the South American stepped forward. "Gee, thanks, gentlemen. I really wanted to get your plug, Carnelito. But we already knew he wouldn't show up. Either way, we've got you two." He stood up and waited while other agents frisked them. Then handcuffed them and lifted them up. "I mean, I do deals," he said. "That is if you can give me something worth more then yourselves."

Neither one of them spoke. Juggernot was placed in the front SUV, while Mishna was placed in the back. The guy pulled his phone back out and made another call. Then ten minutes later, other DEA vehicles pulled up.

***

The call woke Inez out of her sleep. She held the phone to her ear and listened. A few words were said on her end and the call ended. She'd first met Agent Hernandez through Swan. Inez happened to be in the car once when Swan was pulled over and had crack in the car, but Swan took the charge. After a drug test proved that Inez didn't smoke. She didn't have to worry about it. Then Agent Hernandez would pop up from time to time. Not asking anything. He was just there, and Inez realized that Swan was giving them information. They eventually came at her saying her salon was paid for by drug money.

That was the first time she told on anyone. She'd given them Brian. After that, it was several more dope boys, but it was never enough. She knew they would keep coming back. Then Agent Hernandez came to her one day and told her that Jugggernot knew about Mishna. Even showed her pictures of Pipe sitting in his car watching whatever hotel they were in.

Agent Hernandez then somehow got his hands on a copy of divorce papers Juggernot's lawyer was working on. Showing her how he was about to divorce her. At that point, Inez made her deal. She even recorded it so they couldn't trick her. She'd give them both Mishna and Juggernot if they let her keep her cars, house, and salon, and wouldn't ask her to snitch on anyone else. That was her deal, she had it all on tape.

Chapter Fourteen

"I had to hustle, my back to the wall, ashy knuckles, pockets filled with a lot of lint. Not a cent/gotta vent, lot of innocent lives lost on the project bench. Whatchu hollerin'? Gotta pay rent, bring dollars in." Jay-Z: Renegade

The news about Mishna and Juggernot was all over the T.V. Every station had something about the drug bust. It was said they were caught with fifty Kilos of cocaine and an undisclosed amount of money. The GBI and DEA were heading a major task force. Judges had signed allegedly 101 secret indictments. No one knew who was on their list, but they were all expected to be rounded up before the end of the week.

***

The first call didn't surprise him. After he and Jasmine watched the news coverage. They were sitting in her living room where she was packing her things. The new house they were moving into was in the Hepzibah, Georgia area. On Brookstone Drive. It was pretty big, it had four bedrooms, a living/dining room, den, pantry, and a large back yard. Francis had written a check to buy the house straight out.

They were waiting for the Real Estate agent to call confirming the check clearance, but they weren't worried. He'd already called Mrs. Brant and asked if he would clear. The Bank manager told him he could probably buy two or three houses without worrying. So, they decided to pack her things first. Then they would go over and pack his. When the phone rung he answered on the third ring.

"Yeah."

"Rude, I need yer help, Star," Mishna said.

"What you want me to do, Star?"

"Listen, Rude, go see my lawyer. They haven't given me a bail yet. But I need you to secure the lawyer for me. I'll put the funds back as soon as I'm out. We cool on that, Star?" he asked.

Francis wanted to say no, but couldn't, there was always an un-spoken bond between Jamaicans. Especially when in the states. Because everyone from the islands was in a foreign land.

"I'll pull up on him, Star," he said.

Then he took the lawyer's name down. Jasmine didn't say anything. She just continued packing, then the second call came. This one really shook them up.

"Yeah?" Francis said.

"Yo, I'm in the bing, Pa," Young Castro's voice came.

Francis suddenly became serious. "What you need me to do, bruh?" he asked.

The bond between him and Young Castro had grown to the extent where they were like brothers. It didn't seem like there was anything he wouldn't do for the younger man. All he had to do was ask.

"Yo, is your Earth there? Put the phone on speaker. A'ight, *peace Queen*," he said.

"Peace. What can I do to help?" Jasmine asked. She also had developed a bond with Young Castro and Raine.

"I need you to find my Queen. Tell her to go get that dough outta her box. She'll know what's up. Tell her to come down here and be ready to get me out," he said.

"So, they giving you bail?" Francis asked.

"Yeah, yeah, Pa. The Jakes ain't even come to get me. They was pulling up on Cream and Dawg. But they thought they lived at my spot," he explained. "Son, they kicked the door in and found me wit' a lot of that good smelling stuff," he said.

"How much?" Francis asked.

"I'm just under Fed time, Pa, but I don't know if the state gon' trip."

Francis was thinking he might be okay as long as it was weed, and it wasn't enough to be federal.

***

Jasmine went with Raine as she stopped at her bank and got some money out of her safety deposit box. Then they went to get Young Castro out. At the jail, they were told that he was given a bail instead of a fine. Jasmine explained that meant that the state was going to charge him. The only good thing was a good lawyer could keep it out of court for a while. Young Castro had never been convicted of a crime. He wouldn't go to prison, but he might get probation.

"Yo', Ma, I'm not worried about no probation. I've gotta get my business in order. I might lose two of my soldiers. And I just lost all my smell good."

Jasmine was driving, with Raine in the passenger seat. While Young Castro was in the back seat smoking the vanilla Raine gave him.

"Will you be able to get them out?" Raine asked.

"Nah, Ma, word is the judge ain't doing no bonds on those secret indictments. My Sons gon' do some time. Plus, they got hit wit' some work on em," he was stressing in the back seat. "But it ain't no sweat and I'ma keep they books fat. Which reminds me, Ma. Did you put that on their books like I asked you?"

"Yep, I put a grand on each one," Raine said.

"Good, it'll hold 'em for a minute. I'ma shortstop one of these lawyers tomorrow. Ayo, Big Sis, you know any good lawyers?" he asked

"I already called someone while we were waiting on you to get released," Jasmine said. "We've got to stop by there now. That's where we're going."

"Damn, Big Sis, I appreciate the love," he said.

***

In the end, Young Castro had to pay the lawyer forty-thousand to take all three cases.

"I'll be straight up with you," Diane Alexandria said. "I may be able to make this disappear. The marijuana charge, but it'll cost you a bit," the lawyer said.

"How much is a bit?" Young Castro asked.

"Well, it's just marijuana, and you've never been convicted of a crime. To make it go away completely, it would cost you about a hundred grand. But that's with no court appearance and no judge involved," she said.

"Done," Young Castro said. "And yo, you get that done. I'll give you another hundred as a retainer. Plus, I'ma pay you to take my boy's cases. How that sound?"

All three of them watched as Diane smile. "It sounds to me like you have a lawyer. But a bit of advice, try not to get caught with that much stuff again."

***

As soon as they left Diane's firm. She placed a call to Chief District Attorney Lloyd Sullivan Grant's office. Where she spoke with him about his daughter's friend.

"And he's going to pay you the hundred grand?" Lloyd asked.

"He's bringing it to me tomorrow," she said. There was a moment of silence.

"So, you want this case thrown away?" he asked.

"Well, seeing as the search warrant wasn't for him. And whoever applied for it didn't have the right information. An argument, I'll also be using in his two friend's cases," she said. "I don't see why it would be a problem."

"Uh-huh, and just what do I get out of the deal?"

"About forty-thousand and a date," she said seductively.

"Depends, will you be wearing those little frilly thongs you usually wear?" he asked.

"It's possible, you'll just have to wait and see." She ended the call.

The case would disappear and she could focus on the other two. The affair between her and Lloyd had been going on for quite some time, but it wasn't an all-out affair. After all, they were both married. So, they were extra careful.

***

Several of the major drug dealers were picked up in all the madness. Among those picked up were also Ace, Dap, Lil' Henry, and some more from Old Savannah Road. Easy Money and his boy Good Brakes were picked up with half the Southside crew. Along with so many from Sunset that it was hard to tell who wasn't picked up. Because most of them were in hiding. *The Bottom* also lost a good many of its dealers. In all, of the 101 Secret indictments that were reported, ninety-six of those people were in jail.

Agent Conklyn leaned back in his chair with his hands laced behind his head and his feet kicked up on his desk, smoking a Marlboro. He had to give it to Agent Hernandez. Even though, he'd fucked up and lost the best snitch they'd ever had. Him letting her get their deal on tape and having a lawyer bring it by the office for them to listen to. She proved to be a smart bitch.

Yet, she'd come through like a champ. Not only with Mishna and Juggernot. But ninety of the names indicted were names of drug dealers that women talked about in her salon. The smart bitch didn't even know her place was bugged. So, she could stop snitching. As long as she continued to gossip. They'd still get their information.

***

Inez was able to breathe easy. She'd just come from her lawyers, the FBI wouldn't be bothering her. Thanks to her tape. On top of that, it was a good thing that Juggernot had everything except his bank account in her name. Which, with the tape, the Feds weren't going to try and take. Her lawyer even got it to where she wouldn't have to testify against anyone in court.

She did hate to lose Mishna, though. The nigga had some good dick, but it didn't matter. She'd already had her eyes on another up and coming young hustler. A young nigga out of Sunset called *Killa Black*. She had been getting gas at the Citgo gas station one day and the young hustler pulled up in his Nissan Rogue.

He'd tried to get her number, but she refused. He was no more than twenty-three, while here she was about to be forty soon. She did know where he hustled. Since that day she'd seen him several times and with Juggernot and Mishna locked up. She would definitely need a new dick supply. Maybe she needed to find another backup just in case. It couldn't hurt, to have more than one dick on standby.

Chapter Fifteen

Big Dredd called just as they were getting onto the boat, the call didn't last long. All he said was that he would have someone meet him when he reached St. Thomas. The boat was one of the boats that Francis owned. It was a Yacht that was built in 2001. It had a gourmet galley, three staterooms, and three heads. Custom tall Carbon rig, bow thruster, hydraulic winches/furlers, and all control lines within reach of the helm. The inside was highly glossed cherry wood interior.

"Ayo, listen, Pa." Francis was standing on the deck as the captain took the boat out of the Miami Marina. He held a Corona, Young Castro had a Heineken when he came up. "Son, I've never been on a fuckin' boat before. Yo' this shit is bananas, Pa," he was saying.

Jasmine and Raine were still down below. When he last checked they were putting on bathing suits.

"You know, there's something I've been meaning to talk to you about. I just hadn't had the time," he said.

"Well, shit, what's the science? We ain't got nothing but time until we reach St. Thomas." Young Castro smiled.

Francis thought silently as he looked out across the waters before them.

"I've been thinking, it might be good if you fell back out of the streets. Maybe manage the club or something. You know, sort of fall back out of the spotlight," Francis said.

Young Castro laughed. Francis couldn't see what he said that was so funny.

"Yo, my bad, Pa. For a minute, I thought you were serious or some shit," he said, noticing that Francis wasn't laughing. "Ayo, you serious? Yo', Son, how a nigga gon' eat if he can't hustle? Shit, yo' club spot ain't gon' bring in that much loot. I mean it's good money, but Pa," he tried to express his thoughts.

The girls finally came up on deck. They laid their towels out and sat down, rubbing sunscreen on as they were about to lay in the Sun.

"Nah, you misunderstood what I was saying," Francis told him. "What I'm saying is this, with both Cream and Dawg about to do Fed time. That only leaves your man, Poe, right?"

"True, true, Poe's holding shit down," Young Castro said.

"A'ight, imagine this. Let's say you get two more niggas and put them in position. Since the Feds came through on those secret indictments. They left a whole lot of empty shoes to be filled," Francis outlined.

"Exactly my point, why a nigga can't stop hustling. Pa, there is too much money out there unspoken for."

"But what if you could get it, without niggas knowing you the one getting it?" Francis suggested. "What if you could set three niggas up to be King Pins or whatever they wanna call themselves. But the point is, they really work for you. All their work comes from you. What if you could do that. But at the same time, people only saw you as the manager of the club. Nobody seeing your real moves," Francis explained.

He waited while Young Castro thought it over. "It's a good dream while it lasted, Son. But I just lost two guys and all my smell good. I was hoping to ask you to fuck wit' me until I get right. Plus, I spent some major cake with that lawyer," Young Castro told him. Then it was quiet for a moment. "Besides, a nigga ain't got them type of connects, Pa. Even if you fuck wit' me on the smell good. A nigga still gon' need a coke connect," he added.

"So, if you had a cocaine connection, you think you could do it?" Francis asked.

He was pretty sure Big Dredd knew some people in that business. Even if he wasn't into the cocaine trade anymore. He would still be able to plug him into someone who was.

"Yeah, yeah I could do that, Pa. I could bring two niggas down from Brooklyn. Put them on, it could be done," he said.

That was the end of the conversation for then. Francis pulled his Galaxy out and sent a text to Big Dredd. There was no more talk about hustling at all. He would have to wait.

***

Mishna walked over to the payphones that lined the wall. Rabbi had spoken with his lawyer and made sure he had money on his books. The Feds came to ask him questions several times. All his assets that were known by his name, were frozen. He dropped the change into the phone and dialed a number.

"Hello?" Angel answered on the first ring.

"Hey, Queen. How you been?" he asked.

"Fine, but what took you so long to call me?"

"Been talking to my lawyer and these F.B.I muthafuckas. I'm tryin' to see my way out this shit. But the road looks dark baby," he explained.

"Oh, I thought you was on the phone wit' one of yo' other bitches," she said.

"Don't be like that, baby. Right now, I ain't got nobody in my corner. Don't you turn on me, too," he said.

"Nah, nigga, I got you. I just didn't wanna be nobody's fool. So, tell me what's up?" she said.

Mishna told her everything that happened. How the whole thing went down. Angel was also going to school for criminal law. So, she had a head for details and it seemed she asked all the same questions the lawyer asked. They stayed on the phone for at least an hour. It was a good thing there were several more phones mounted on the wall. It seemed most of these niggas didn't have money to use them. Or didn't have anybody to call. Either way, he spent the hour romancing Angel. Making sure she was still on his team.

***

Noel saw the text and had to read it twice. He'd told Rabbi to steer clear of the crack game. He did everything he could to make sure he didn't have to get into it. However, this text was as clear as day. He and his people were on their way down to St. Thomas. He wanted to know if he still had snow skiing buddies. Because he needed to meet one. Then he asked for him to get back at him the first chance he could.

Noel sat the phone down, then picked up pages of a book he was reading. It was written by this young brother who was also locked up, but the book was unpublished. The brother didn't have any outside help so he couldn't make it happen and he wrote some good material. Noel had been reading his work for some time now. The guys' name was Trai 'Quan, and the book he was reading now was called *The Pain Of My Tears*.

He finished the chapter, then picked his phone back up and made a call.

***

"Stop, drop, shut 'em down open up shop, oh, no, that's how Ruff Riders roll!" ~DMX~

Poe pulled up in his cocaine white Durango with the music blasting. He was supposed to have been moving down O.S. and setting up shop, but with the GBI coming through snatching up both Cream and Dawg. Young Castro had to put O.S. on hold for the moment. So, Poe was holding down 8th and Grand by himself. He slowed the truck down and looked around.

"The fuck this nigga at?" he stressed to himself.

Having gotten the call while he was in the midst of talking to one of the young girls at Mcdonalds. He'd been about to get the number of the one he'd been shooting at. Then this nigga Pat called. Talking about he needed a hook up bad. Nigga said he had $600 on deck. Poe was never one to turn down some dough. Just when he was about to say fuck it and head back to the Mcdonalds. He heard the whistle, seeing as he'd turned the music down. Poe turned his head and looked out of the passenger window. He saw, Pat—but he heard—

"What's up, Thug? You remember me!"

When he turned to look back out of the driver's side window, he saw Pete Rose standing there holding a Glock 22.

"What the fuck?" Poe fell over to the passenger seat.

Pete Rose pushed forward with the barrel of the gun inside the Durango and emptied the clip. The whole scene went down in under five minutes. When the gun stopped making noise, the only sound heard was feet on the pavement, running away from the crime scene. Poe wasn't dead, though. He was in pain and was having trouble breathing. Somehow he managed to get his iPhone out and press 911.

"Nine-one-one, what's your emergency?"

"Been—been—shot—bad."

"Sir, I can barely hear you. Did you say you've been shot?" the woman asked.

Poe couldn't say anything else, he'd blacked out.

"Sir, Sir, can you hear me?"

The 911 operator ran a trace on the phone's GPS. Just as the call was tracked, another 911 call came in and a woman was reporting the shooting. The operator dispatched an ambulance and police to the scene. The cell phone was still on. It seemed like she could still hear the guy trying to breathe.

"Sir, stay with me an ambulance is on the way. If you can hear me. Just hold on," she said.

Then she ran a check on the phone. It was registered to someone name, Parker Evans. She then ran the name through the quick search at DMV. She saw that he drove a Dodge Durango which was fairly new.

"Mr. Evans, the ambulance is almost there. Just hold on," she said.

Not long after saying that she heard the emergency response team as they arrived. Poe didn't die, they were able to stabilize him until getting him to the hospital. He'd been hit eight times in various places. The most serious was the ones to his Digestive system, arteries, and kidney. Because he'd fallen sideways, most of the bullets entered his waist, side, back, and shoulder, missing the spine by very little.

Trai'Quan

Chapter Sixteen

They arrived at the Frentown Marina in St. Thomas, which was only about ten minutes away from the St. Thomas airport. The Captain pulled Francis to the side and explained to him the details of his Catamarans Yachts. Then said that he should have the other's wait while he went to meet his staff. Francis did just that. Except he told them if they went exploring to meet back at the boat in one hour. Then he went with the Captain to meet the people, Big Dredd had in charge. The people who now worked for him.

***

Mishna stood at the sink washing the blood off his face. He'd just gotten jumped by four guys who came to rob him for his store goods. His eye was swollen, he suspected his nose was broken and his lip was busted. Other than that he thought there might be a broken rib or two, but he would live. The niggas took his store. Not that he really cared. What hurt him the most was his pride. Mishna had never been in an environment like this one before.

In Trinidad, he'd grown up in the roughest sections. He and Rabbi had fought the biggest bullies to survive. But over the years he hadn't had so much as a fight in the streets. So, when they came at him for his store goods, he wasn't ready. Four against one was a cowards' way anyway. He should have been able to take the first two that came through the door. He was out of shape and in front he was overweight, and there was still some time until his Federal court date.

Mishna made up his mind, he didn't have any friends. Juggernot was in another section of the jail. Even if he wasn't, could he count on the nigga to help him? Mishna already suspected the nigga knew he was fucking his wife, but it didn't matter. Starting today, he was gon' workout every day. Push-ups, pull-ups, back and arms, and sit-ups. He would eat what food they gave him. Not spending his money on store, and next time he went to the store, he would be ready. He wondered if Rabbi had gone through the same shit, and he did twenty years.

***

They got two suites at the St. Thomas resort, the rooms were lavish. They almost looked like apartments or condos. Francis had to pay for both rooms since he seemed to be the one with the money. After they showered and changed. They met outside the rooms and went to the resort's restaurant downstairs.

"Ayo, Pa, let me tell you. This vacation is truly bananas. Yo', Son! I love you, Pa," Young Castro said.

"Don't worry about it, bruh. Since I own these boats I imagine we'll be coming down here more often."

"Nigga, say word."

The waiter came and took their orders. He also ordered the D'Ambonnay 1996 which was $2,195 a bottle.

"Damn, nigga. You've got money to burn, huh?" Raine asked.

She and Jasmine enjoyed their drinks, and it was at that point Francis reached into his pocket and pulled out the black ring box. He placed in on the table right in front of Jasmine.

"Oh, my God! Girl, this nigga fixin' to ask you to marry him." Raine turned her flute glass up and refilled it.

Jasmine picked up the box and opened it. The ring inside held a 2ct centerpiece diamond with five smaller diamonds forming a crescent around it. Francis had paid $26,000 for the ring.

"Look, this ain't no romance movie. So, a nigga ain't getting down on his knee." He smiled. "Nah, seriously. You want to do this or what?" he asked.

Jasmine smiled. "Of course, I do."

He took the ring out of the box and placed it on her hand. Then she held it up to look at it.

"Oohhh!" Raine said, then looked at Young Castro. "Ahem, so tell me. What I got to do to get one of those?"

"Shit, Ma, it ain't you," he said "Remember, I just took a hit. Let a nigga get his pockets right. And you gon' see yours," he promised.

"Speaking of getting yo' pockets right. " Francis pulled his Galaxy out and checked his messages.

"We've got to meet this guy in two hours."

"Yo, word. What's the deal?" Young Castro asked.

"Just chill, we'll find out when we meet again." Francis didn't know *who* he was. He'd just received the text from someone who said Noel asked him to call. Since he was in the Caribbean, they could meet in two hours. Francis had just confirmed it and the guy sent the location of the meeting.

***

"Ayo Thug, I appreciate you looking out on that move," Pete Rose said.

He and Pat were standing next to their rides at the gas station in front of Williamsburg.

"Don't worry about it, Thug. I wasn't feeling them New York niggas anyway," Pat said.

"Yeah, I just wish we could have robbed the nigga first," Pete Rose said.

They were still talking when the Lincoln MKS Sedan that was baby blue sitting on 22-inch Armano rims pulled up beating hard.

"Rolling down the street smoking 'N' doe sippin' on gin and juice. Laid back, with my mind on my money and money on my mind."

They watched as Jeeta stepped out wearing color dye baby blue Timberlands, Roca Wear jeans, and a Carolina Panthers Tee. A female exited the passenger side also rocking the colors hard. She wore a Carolina Panther's 4XL Jersey like it was a dress, with powder blue Prada heels and a lot of jewelry.

"Sup, Rose, Pat?" Jeeta said.

The girl pulled out her blue Donna Karen bag and went to the gas station while Jeeta pumped the gas.

"What's up, Jeeta. I see you Crippin' hard," Pete Rose said, his area was Gangsta Disciples.

"Something like that." Jeeta pumped the gas, then as if he had an afterthought. "Say, you, niggas hear 'bout homie, Poe getting shot the other day?"

"Oh, yeah, yeah. But I don't know who killed him," Pete Rose said.

Jeeta gave both of them a hard look. He couldn't say, but he suspected these marks knew something. Not many knew that Poe was Crippin'.

"Nah, Cuz ain't die, but he's in critical condition, though. I'm just trying to find out who touched him like that," Jeeta said.

He watched as they both hunched their shoulders. He finished pumping the gas at about the same time Crystal came back out.

"Ayo, I'ma holla." He threw up the deuces. Then he got in the Sedan and pulled off.

They were quiet for a minute.

"Damn, that bitch ass nigga ain't die?" Pete Rose said.

"And the nigga a Crip," Pat said. "More than likely he was representing Jeeta's hood. Seeing as Jeeta was interested in what happened."

***

"What do you think, baby?" Crystal asked.

Jeeta thought about it some more. He and her were from California. They'd come East together some years ago. Neither one fucked with a lot of people. They did fuck with Young Castro and his crew hard. Because all of them were down with the Crips, they just didn't go out the way to stress it real hard.

"Yeah, them niggas some marks," he said.

From the description, they received from a crackhead off 8th and Grand. Pete Rose was the one doing the shooting. Jeeta knew Young Castro was out of town. So, he would wait until he came back.

***

The Caribbean Island form a 1500-mile long, 2400 km Archipelaop, The Antilles, separates the Caribbean Sea from the Mexican Gulf. The islands consist of Cuba, Jamaica Hispaniola, Haiti, Dominican Republic, and Puerto Rico. The U.S. Virgin Islands consist of Jamaica, Trinidad, Bermuda, Belize, Guyana, St. Thomas, and others. They had to take a boat to St. Vincent Island, which was known for having two distinct complexions of people. One was black, the other a reddish-yellow coloring. This was a result of African slaves mixing with the Native Indians of St. Vincent Island.

Francis and Young Castro stepped out of the boat and were led to the Marina's main office. When they stepped inside, they were standing before an older reddish-yellow complexed man with long dreads. He wore baggy shorts and an island button-up shirt.

"You must be, Rabbi?" The man stepped forward to shake his hand. "Noel has spoken highly of you. He gives you much praise." He looked to the younger man. "And you?"

"People call me, Young Castro," he said.

"Well, any friend of Noel's is a friend of mine," the man said. "By the way, my name is, Carnelito Guani. My first name means brother in Spanish. While my last name in Mandinka means Gold. Thus, I'm either the brother of Gold or the Golden Brother." He smiled. "People say it's because my family has reddish, golden skin."

He waved them to sit on the couch, while he went over behind the counter. He made three drinks. Then came back around and brought them theirs. He went back to get his.

"Noel tells me, he's surprised to see you've decided to enter the cocaine trade. He said that he didn't want this for you," Carnelito said.

"Oh, I'm not," Francis explained. "My little brother here is, I'm simply sponsoring him."

"Ah, so, your word carries him?"

"Exactly," Francis said, watching as Carnelito examined Young Castro closely.

"Okay, my young friend. What is it you want to do?" Carnelito asked finally.

"Well, I ain't never had a direct connection before. And I've only been able to buy a few keys at a time," Young Castro said.

"Let me stop you right there, young man," Carnelito said. "How about I tell what I need as a representative in the states? And we'll just work from there."

Chapter Seventeen

"Street dreams are made of these niggas, push Beamers and 300 Es. A drug dealer's destiny is reaching a key. Everybody is looking for something." Nas: Street Dreams

"No, Pa. No, this can't be fucking happening to me," Young Castro cried out.

Francis stood right next to him, listening as the doctor told him how they were barely able to save Poe's life, but they had. They didn't bring Jasmine and Raine with them because neither knew what to expect. They'd received the news as soon as they returned home.

"All my Soldiers have fallen, Son. Just when shit is about to get right. A nigga feels like he's got devil's luck," Young Castro said.

Upon meeting with Carnelito the older man had given Young Castro a deal he couldn't refuse. Since he'd lost so many of his representatives in the states. He was able to give Young Castro a million dollar startup deal for $200,000. Due to the loss, he'd just suffered before the trip. When he had looked over at Francis he caught the slight head nod. Francis was giving him the $200,000. Carnelito even said that he would get the cocaine into the states and Young Castro would receive a call once it arrived.

"Look," Francis started. "Ain't no use crying about what you can't change. Didn't you say you could bring some other people from upstate down here?"

"Yeah, no doubt. I could bring a whole army if I need it."

"Nah, all you need is three or four solid niggas," Francis said.

Young Castro took a deep breath calming himself down. "A'ight, Pa, I can do this. Let me go make arrangments for my nigga Poe. I'll be back, Son."

Francis stood there and watched as he walked away. Thinking that the younger man would definitely become rich if he kept his head on his shoulders. Just as he had that particular thought, his Galaxy vibrated against his thigh. He pulled it out, and wasn't expecting the message that had just come through in a text, it read:

//: You need to see Ms. Sheba.

***

"You know the most beautiful thing about locking up a hundred drug dealers under a Federal Indictment," Agent Conklyn said to Agent Hernandez and the Federal District Attorney Susan Rothchild. Not of the Rothchild banking family.

"And what is that?" FDA Rothchild asked.

Agent Conklyn to share a smile. "You get at least fifty snitches," he said.

Lying on the desk in front of them were about fifty affidavits. All pointing fingers at other drug dealers.

"And how many of those do you think are factual?" she asked.

Agent Conklyn thought about the affidavits. "About fifteen, and we'll only use about ten," he said.

Most of what he'd already read was information they'd already known. That was because of the wiretap on Inez's Salon, and because some of the things that were said. They would be able to get around the lawyer she had and that tape she'd made. They were waiting to hear back from her lawyer now. Having already called and telling him that they need to see him.

"In any case, a lot of this stuff is state. How are you going to get the States DA to play ball?" she asked.

"Actually, that parts your job. You'll have to go over to his office and sweet talk him into it," Conklyn suggested.

"And, just how am I supposed to do that?" Susan asked.

"It's real easy actually." Conklyn smiled. "Old Lloyd's got a weakness for white flesh. But you haven't had the chance to meet him yet."

Conklyn took the time to look Susan up and down. She was a tall, red-head, with long legs and really nice breasts. *Yeah, Lloyd would play ball,* he thought.

***

When his secretary informed him that the Federal District Attorney was there to see him. Lloyd knew he hadn't seen the woman yet. However, he'd heard that she could be a bitch. So, he was expecting an older woman who wore one-inch-thick glasses and had a slight hunch in her back. But when his secretary opened the door and showed her in. Lloyd started thinking he wanted to play any type of game this woman wanted to play.

***

Jeeta pulled up to Young Castro's driveway almost as soon as Young Castro did. He and Crystal got out, with her wearing a blue and white Coogie with a Fendi blue jean skirt and wedges by Prada that were also blue. Jeeta wore Sean John jeans and an Avirex USA XL shirt with blue and white Air Force Ones.

"Ayo, what's the deal, Son?" Young Castro asked as he stepped outside.

He gave Crystal a hug then told her Raine was inside.

"What's up, Cuz?" Jeeta asked.

Officially, Young Castro wasn't a Crip. He wasn't apart of any gang. While both Poe and Cream were Jeeta"s homies because they both were.

"You see lil homie, Poe, yet?" Jeeta asked.

Young Castro sat on the steps with a deep sigh. "Yeah, I been up there not long ago, Pa. I made sure they gon' give him the best care. This shit is crazy, Son."

"So, what's crackin', Cuz? You down to straighten this shit up or what?" Jeeta asked.

This caused Young Castro to look up. "Yo,' Son, just give me a name and that muthafucka gon' damn sure rest in peace. Just a name, Pa, that's all I need," Young Castro pleaded.

"The nigga, Pete Rose, and that nigga he be with who got them thick ass waves in his head," Jeeta said.

"That's that jealous ass nigga, Pat," Young Castro said as he heard it. "Yo, they the ones did it?"

"Yeah. So, what you wanna do, Cuz?" Jeeta asked.

He hadn't made his plans to go back to New York yet. Now that Jeeta was standing in front of him. Young Castro was figuring him into the picture. Poe would be alright in a few weeks. The doctor said there wouldn't be any serious damage. The package he had on him when he got shot somehow came up missing. He suspected the cops put it in their pockets.

"Come on, Pa, let's see about these marks," he said.

Afterward, he would pull Jeeta over about the business.

***

This time he was ready for them. Mishna had brought twelve can sodas and put them inside of his pillowcase. He tied a knot into it and sat it by the door. The idiots didn't know what all he'd gotten from the store. They just knew that he had a large bag. The fools didn't come immediately they waited. He fixed himself a bowl of soup and got on the phone for thirty minutes. Then he stood at the TV eating his soup while watching the news. When the news went off and some sitcom came on, he turned and walked back to his room.

Mishna suspected that it would be going down soon. He could just feel the energy. From the corner of his eye, he saw the four robbers as they stood up and merged into one group. As soon as he pulled his door open, he reached in and grasped the pillowcase. Then he turned with his first swing. The first one to get hit went out cold.

"Oh, shit!"

Another one tried to sidestep, but Mishna caught him square in the face, shattering his nose. The third one tried to rush him and Mishna broke his jaw. He had to chase the last one. The nigga almost made it to his room, too.

Then the double doors to the floor slid open.

"*Hey, put the bag down!*" the guards shouted as they ran on to the range.

Mishna wasn't about to let this fool get away. He swung and connected with the side of his head just as he grabbed the room door to try and close it. Not only did he send the nigga down, but the nigga started to shake like he was a fish out of water. Mishna stood there with the pillowcase in his hands, looking. The officers also stopped and watched. Then the nigga's body locked up and he went completely still. Mishna dropped the bag and a tear rolled from his eye. He knew he'd just gotten himself a murder charge.

***

"Damn," Juggernot cursed out loud. He'd just gotten word that Mishna killed his cousin Nate with a bag of sodas.

When he had first come up with the plan to have Nate and his partners rob Mishna and beat him up. He hadn't thought that the nigga would fight back. Not that hard for his store. But he hadn't told them to rob him the second time. They must have assumed the nigga was a free pick and decided to doo-wop. Now this nigga done killed his mama's nephew. He didn't know how he was gon' explain that.

Maybe he could act like he didn't have anything to do with it. That was if the nigga didn't run his damn mouth. At least he didn't have to worry about this nigga Mishna anymore. Especially with his lawyer having just told him that they should beat these charges. The stupid ass DEA Agents hadn't actually made a transaction with them. They never passed any drugs in exchange for the money. Which meant they'd given the DEA Agents a gift with the money.

The lawyer said they could expect to be released in a couple of weeks. Well, he would be released. This fool Mishna would be re-charged and this time for murder. Juggernot couldn't help but smile. This pussy ass nigga would never get out of prison. He'd probably end up being somebody's *Bitch* on the inside. That's what the dread-lock wearing muthafucka get. Niggas always trying to be players.

***

"In the hood, the summertime is the killing season it's hot out this bitch, that's a good enough reason!"

Pat was sitting in his Nissan Maxima at the stoplight bobbing his head to tunes of 50 Cent's song. There was a pizza delivery truck in front of him. The system he'd just had put in at the Kicker Sound System store sounded damn good. He hadn't even turned it all the way up, yet. Right now, it was only on number 4 on the volume dial and it was still loud. In fact, it was so loud that Pat didn't notice the dark blue Buick that pulled up behind him.

Jeeta opened the door and stepped out on the passenger side. He glanced around, then turned to walk to the front of the Buick, where he crossed over to the driver's side. When he reached the driver's door of the Nissan, he saw Pat bobbing his head. Jeeta waited until Pat noticed him standing there.

Kha! Chik! The twenty-gauge pistol grip pump was cocked and loaded.

"Oh, shit!" Pat screamed.

"*I've seen gangstas get religious when they start bleedin'. Saying Lord Jesus help me cause they ass leakin'*!" 50 Cent continued to rap in the background.

Everything happened within the space of ten seconds. A pregnant pause, then the second of the shotgun blast came. The sound seemed to come back.

Booommm! The twenty-gauge spit. *Kha! Chik*! He cocked it again. *Booommm*! The first blast more than likely killed him, but the second one made sure he was dead.

***

Raine waited the required time, then she checked the stick and saw the plus sign on it. The sign itself indicated that she was pregnant.

"Damn, I'm gon' kill that nigga and his dick when he gets home," she said

Not that she had a problem having another baby. Their son Casey was about to be two-years-old. The thing was, aside from working at the club at night. She was just about to get into Augusta State

College. She'd just taken the test and intended to major in Financing and Computers, now this nigga gon' get her pregnant.

"Yeah, nigga, this one here gon' get me a ring and a new house out there where Jasmine lives," she said.

Having already told Young Castro that it would be best if they moved off 8th and Grand. Considering all the violence and drug dealing going on. She really didn't think it would be a good place to raise their son. The only reason she was even there was because Young Castro owned the house that they lived in. She definitely didn't want to live in the projects, but he'd taken that loss. All of the money they had saved up for other things, he'd had to use it.

She knew too that Francis had given him $200,000 to complete this deal. So, she was about to push for him to sell the house. If he needed to borrow what else, he needed from Francis. She fully intended to move within the next two weeks. She would give him about a month on the ring. She'd wait until he got the package and start moving it. Then she wanted her ring.

"Yeah, nigga, that's what's up," she said to the pregnancy stick that she still held in her hand.

***

It was late when the phone rang, awaking Conklyn out of a peaceful sleep. He looked beside him and saw that his wife was still asleep. Nothing could wake her once she went down. He rubbed his eyes, then reached to the bedside table where his phone lay.

"Hello," he said, still sleepy.

"I've got some good news, and I have bad news. Which would you like to hear first?" Susan Rothchild asked.

"Give me the good news," he said.

"Grant's going to play ball our way," she said.

Conklyn wondered if she'd sucked his dick or just given him the whole trip.

"And the bad news?" he asked.

"There's one on your list we can't have. This guy's a friend of his daughter. So, unless you actually catch the guy holding a kilo of coke or crack. We can't touch him, and that's nothing under a kilo," she explained.

He knew that Lloyd's daughter had some friends in certain circles. So, he wasn't shocked by it.

"Shit, well, who the fuck is this guy?" He asked.

"His name's, Casey Porter. Alias, Young Castro," she said.

"Fuck!" Conklyn cursed.

"What, did I miss something?" she asked.

"He's the guy most of them are snitching on—" He paused trying to think. "And you say Grant won't deal on him?"

"He said no deals. If you get this guy it had better be a Federal case and red-handed. He's not even going to go for conspiracy. But trafficking and possession, yeah. Take it or leave it," she explained and waited while he appeared to be thinking about the deal, she'd just laid out to him. "Listen, you've still got all the others. If I were you, I'd take this deal. It's the best you've got," she told agent Conklyn. "But I need an answer, right now."

Conklyn wondered if she were still with Lloyd at the very moment, probably sucking his dick as she spoke.

"We'll take it, I'll start the process first thing in the morning," he said. The call ended. '*Young Castro,*' he thought. Most of the snitches had his name in their mouths. Then too, not one of them gave anything solid or factual.

***

"Where the fuck is this nigga?" Pete Rose asked as he ended the call. He'd been trying to call Pat's phone for the past ten minutes.

At that moment he was sitting inside of the Waffle House. Which was where they were supposed to meet. That was over ten minutes ago, and this nigga wasn't answering his phone. He looked up and smiled as the waitress walked by. She'd been flirting with him the whole time he'd been in there. Her name tag read, Cynthia. She was an older woman, about thirty-seven, but she was fine.

The bitch was a red-bone, with thick thighs. He could tell because her uniform was tight, and it seemed like she loved bending over to clean the tables a little too much. Pete saw her glance back several times. Checking to see that he was looking. He wasn't being shy about it either. He checked the time on his phone.

Yeah, this nigga was definitely late. Pete Rose was about to try the number again when the car pulled up to the window where he sat. What made it so strange was the person driving it had the high beams on and the light was nearly blinding. There were several people inside and they all took notice. Even the two Police officers who seemed to be on their break. Pete Rose watched as the passenger side door opened and it seemed like someone stepped out carrying a bat or an iron pipe in their hand.

Then he thought, '*No, not a bat nor iron pipe.*' "Oh, shit!"

***

Jeeta smiled as he saw the look in Pete Rose's eyes then he cocked the pump.

Kha! Chik!

Then Young Castro stepped out with the street sweeper. It seemed like all hell broke loose. For a full sixty seconds, they pumped shell after shell, bullet after bullet into the Waffle House window. The intention was to kill Pete Rose at all costs. When the shooting stopped they saw Pete Rose's body slumped in the seat. Jeeta calmly turned and got back into the Buick. Young Castro had already slid back in behind the wheel. He backed the car out and turned into the highway.

Then he thought to speak, "Listen, Pa, wit' Cream and Dawg locked up. And my nigga Poe out of action for a minute. I've got a job opening," Young Castro said as he drove. "From where I'm sitting, Son. You qualify as a thug. So, are you interested in a job?"

Jeeta thought it over, if Young Castro was offering him a job then that could only mean major dough.

"Yeah, gon' head and run it down to me, Cuz," he said.

As he drove, Young Castro explained the details. At first, Jeeta was thinking that maybe Young Castro had big dreams. Because he spoke of having a large amount of cocaine one day. But he didn't say when that day would be. Jeeta being a realist, assumed Young Castro was making plans for something he would do in the future. Either way, he decided to ride it out and see what happened.

Chapter Eighteen

"Ayo' D' what up D', Yous' a smooth nigga, I saw you when no-body knew who pulled the trigger. Yeah, you know, it's always over dough. You sure? I could have sworn that it was over a hoe." DMX: Damian

"What in the fuck you mean they can get around the tape?" Inez asked as she sat across the desk from her lawyer.

A well-respected white guy in his 50s. She'd paid him $10,000 to represent her in concerns to her situation with the F.B.I. Thus far everything was going good. Especially with her having copies of the tape.

The lawyer sighed, trying to find the right way to explain to her the legal ramifications of Federal Conspiracy. "They've had your salon bugged for quite some time. So, they have you partaking in all types of conversations. Two, in particular, they may pursue you about. One being the murder of this homosexual," he said.

"But wait a minute I didn't kill that bitch," she stated.

"That maybe so, but it'll be us trying to prove it in court. By some of your conversations alone, you had a lot of motives to want him dead," the attorney explained it to her. "And then there's the tax evasion. They actually went back in your history and pulled that card."

"But wait a minute. I thought it was illegal to bug peoples shit like that?" She said.

Because she simply could not believe this lawyer was telling her that she was about to be fucked by both the IRS and the State for a murder she had nothing to do with.

"Technically," the lawyer said. "But the business with your taxes are a matter of records. And with the murder, they'll just pull all of your friends in. They'll use what they heard on the tapes to trip them up. By the time we reach court. It won't even be a case based on the illegal wiretaps. It'll be your friends snitching on you," he explained to her.

Inez sighed. "So, either way, it goes. I'm a fucked bitch?"

"Unless you agree to help them," he said.

Which was the whole thing, without her, Juggernot would walk free. Even the charges against Mishna would be dropped. All those except for the manslaughter charge they'd given him. That one didn't concern her at all.

"Alright, so what do I have to do?" she asked

"Testify before a Grand Jury. Tell them everything you know about your husband and this other guy."

"I do this—and everything goes away? The IRS, the murder, all of it?" she asked.

The lawyer nodded. Inez bit down on her lip thinking. She just couldn't get away from these people. Ever since she first agreed to snitch. They simply weren't trying to let her get out of the business.

"I want it in writing," she said. "You get it in writing, and I'll do it. Other then that, I'll take my chances."

"I'll let you know tomorrow," the lawyer said.

***

Danial Godfree sighed with relief as the crazy black bitch left his office. Unknown to her, she was about to get them both sent to prison. The FBI found out about some of his shady dealings and pressured him into helping them trick her. He could have easily beat all their bullshit against her. But he couldn't beat the evidence they had against him. Some of it too damaging to even think about. So, he'd made a choice, it was better to throw her under the bus then him.

He had more to lose. All she had to do was tell on a couple of people. So, he'd furthered their cause with the bullshit he just told her. Now he had to make the call. He had to be sure that he was in the clear. He'd done his part.

***

Lloyd was sitting going over issues that needed his attention. He signed papers and documents back to back as his people brought them to him. Mentally his mind was on the time he'd spent with

Susan Rothchild. He really didn't know how to explain his obsession with *White Women*. At one point in his life, he tried to justify it by him being the product of biracial relations himself, but he knew that wasn't it. Lloyd liked the control.

He wasn't a woman beater nor was he into S&M relations or anything. He just got a kick out of having sex with the wealthy successful white women of the world. Those who thought they were too good to be touched by a black dick. There was nothing, absolutely like the feeling he received from cumming all over wealthy white women's faces. It was at those times when he literally felt like *he* was a porn star.

As he sat behind his desk signing papers. All he could think about was his cum plastered all over Susan Rothchilds' pretty face. Her very successful, wealthy pretty white face. Even thinking about it at that moment was giving him an outrageous erection. All she'd wanted was for his office to turn their heads as the Feds played their little games. From what he understood, some of what they wanted to do didn't concern his office anyway. All except the thing with the murder of the homosexual.

He really didn't see this woman Inez as a possible suspect anyway. He pretty much assumed it was a hate crime of some sort. Plus, it happened in a drug-infested area. But, if they wanted to trick the girl into testifying against her husband, that was none of his business. Casey Porter, on the other hand, was a problem. When Susan brought the name up, he immediately remembered the young guy that was Jasmine's friend and that he'd been caught with a nice amount of marijuana. While two of his other friends were caught with crack cocaine.

Jasmine said that he was into some weed. Since he didn't even have an arrest history before then, he believed her. So, some people were snitching on this guy to try and free themselves. On top of all that neither of his friends was snitching. Lloyd knew how the snitch game went. They would say anything to get themselves out of a tight situation. A snitch would even lie or over tell the story. Nobody liked a snitch, even cops hate snitches. While they would make their jobs easy. They were also the lowest scum of the earth.

He made a mental note to give Jasmine a call. To tell her that her friend had some powerful enemies in the streets. That he needed to be careful. He'd give the guy about as much protection as he could. Having told Susan to have her people stand down on this one guy. That if they didn't catch him with a kilo of cocaine or better. Then to leave him alone. He didn't want to see the name, Casey Porter or Young Castro come across his desk for nothing less.

***

Agent Conklyn replaced the phone on its receiver. Having just spoken to the lawyer. He saw no problem with that. His aim was to keep this guy Juggernot from walking. They really weren't worried about Mishna. He would definitely be going to state prison for manslaughter. They'd already talked to Lloyd about the case. The only deal they were accepting was twenty and he'd do ten.

Now they needed to focus on locking the snitch in. Because she was just too valuable to let go. Juggernot hung the phone up and walked back to his room. He couldn't believe the shit his lawyer had just told him. These muthafuckas were charging him with conspiracy. They were preparing to take a witness before the Grand Jury. His lawyer said they weren't releasing the witness's name. For fear of the witness safety. Juggernot couldn't figure out who would turn states witness on him, especially in a conspiracy case.

***

Inez couldn't believe the day she'd had. Between the bullshit with her lawyer, the threats from the F.B.I, and now her having to testify before a Grand Jury. Then her kids came home with problems. She hadn't even opened the salon today. She still needed to get somebody to go through it and find all the bugs the F.B.I had in it. Muthafuckas was listening in on all her good gossip. Well, she thought at least one good thing came out of it all. She'd met her next dick supply at the courthouse.

A thugged out young nigga named, Brutis. He'd been going to pay a fine. When he saw her, he couldn't help but pull over and spit his game in her ear. Being the boss bitch that she was, Inez decided she would make the young nigga famous. Yeah, she would see what the young nigga was talking about. They were going to hook up sometime this weekend. So, yeah good things did happen.

***

As a habit, Inez poured the Carnal Fantasy Intense body soap into the bathtub. It was her favorite scent by Dolce & Gabbana. She then dimmed the lights and removed her robe. Naked, she stepped into the water and leaned back to relax. Both her son and daughter were already in bed. This was usually her quiet time. In the background, *Al Green* was singing in her bedroom. Due to all the shit going on in her life right now. She could use a little comfort. As she laid back in the tub. Her mind began to drift to things other than her problems.

Inez wasn't even aware of the fact that she wasn't alone in the bathroom. She'd never checked the closet where she stored extra towels and face cloths. Had she opened it and stood on her tiptoes. She might have seen the assassin that was folded up on the top shelf like *he* was a towel.

The assassin waited, the door was still cracked from when he'd cracked it earlier. So, he had a good view into the bathroom. He could see that her eyes were closed and her head was lying backward. As the music still played, he was able to unfold himself, without making a sound. Then carefully he lowered his body to the floor. Moving silently and as quietly as he could. He moved out of the closet and soon found himself standing over the woman in the bathtub. Then he bent down and grabbed Inez. Her eyes flew open in a panic.

The assassin was wearing all black, but his face wasn't covered, she knew the face. He had one hand over her mouth so she couldn't scream. She tried to fight him off, he was just too strong. He pushed her head under the water. Inez knew this was her justice for all the wrong she'd done. Just as she knew nobody would come to save her. Nor would anybody miss her when she was gone. She felt her life slipping away slowly. After a while, she stopped struggling and the assassin pressed her all the way to the bottom of the tub. He held her there long enough to be sure she was dead.

When he was sure he retraced his steps. He stopped to look into each kid's room. There wasn't a hit on the kids. He just wanted to be sure that they were asleep, and they were. When he exited the house, he made a point to reactivate the alarm. They didn't want the death to stand out too much.

***

When Ms. Sheba first told him who the target was and that she was the reason for all the drug dealers getting locked up on secret indictments. He'd been surprised, but then there were the tapes of her dealings with the F.B.I to prove it all. As well as, how she'd help set up the fake deal with the person who was supposed to be Carnelito's man but was actually a DEA Agent.

Francis realized that Inez was behind everything. She was even the one who fed Brian to the F.B.I. All of which she did, in her attempts to wiggle out of her own problems. There was a lot of evidence of her cheating on Juggernot. Not that he really cared. Most of it had been with Mishna, though. He wasn't really all that surprised to find that out. Because Mishna loved to brag about how he was out there fucking all of the big dope boys, girls behind their backs.

It was fucking those women that help land his stupid ass in jail. Francis now knew about the manslaughter charge he'd gotten while in the jail. There was nothing he could do about that. However, with Inez out of the picture, that Federal case that they had against him and Juggernot was no longer an issue. Without their witness, the Feds would no longer have a case. That meant even some of those others who'd been arrested on her information would be set free.

Francis assumed that even Cream and Dawg would be freed, too. Which would really be a good thing. He knew that Young

Castro really needed them now. Especially with all the cocaine, he was about to receive from Carnelito soon.

As he made it to the black Cadillac ATS-V Coupe that he drove. Francis was wondering just how many people actually worked for Noel. Because some of the information he got his hands on had to come from someone in the F.B.I., and that wasn't easy to do. As he drove away, he pulled his Galaxy out of his pocket and text Big Dredd.

***

Noel had been reading some updates on his Facebook page when the text came in. He read it, then continued what he was doing. About thirty minutes later he sent a text to someone else. After that, he put his phone up and laid down to sleep. Wondering what the next day would be like.

The End

Book Two:

Animal Thug Preview

Chapter One

"Aaaahhh, God, please—please help me!" the man screamed because of the excruciating pain he was experiencing.

He was tied face forward to the back of a chair, naked. His back was filled with welts, the blood had mixed with the sweat so it was unable to dry up fast. In a way, it seemed to be pouring out of his body. Behind the man, standing with his tank top tee shirt drenched in sweat. Holding the whip in his left hand, looking like he'd once owned an entire plantation of slaves was Poe. He wiped the sweat from his forehead and looked up with a sigh. He glanced over to where the other two men sat.

They were all inside an abandoned warehouse across from the Bethlehem Community Center. It used to be some type of cotton factory or something. Poe couldn't be sure what. Young Castro sat there calmly and quiet as he smoked the Newport cigarette which hung from the corner of his mouth. While Jeeta held his cellphone in hand texting and seemingly he was arguing with himself. Whatever that was about Poe couldn't say and he wasn't about to get into anybody's business.

Instead, he remembered that he had a job to do. Poe drew the whip back and lashed out again. The whip was a traditional Cat – O – nine tails that were made from a thick animal hide. Poe drew it back and flicked it as if *he* was an animal.

"Lord—have mercy—" the man's head came up as he cried out.

At one point in time, he'd also been an animal in the zoo. Inside, it was bothering Poe. Because he'd known this man since their earlier years in New York hustling, running the streets and barking at the moon when they were young thugs. Poe shook his head because it didn't make any sense. When Young Castro first said that he needed them to come down here to August, Georgia to help him. They'd agreed then that they would all stick together. Bonded by the essence of New York city's upbringing, and that nothing would be able to come between them. Poe watched as the new cut he made in Dawg's flesh began to bleed. It sort of made him feel some kind of way.

"Young—please—please just go ahead and kill me!" Dawg pleaded.

When Poe looked over at Young Castro all he saw was Young lighting another Newport off the one that had gotten short. Chain-smoking which he'd been doing since they snatched Dawg up. Even he was wondering why Young Castro didn't just go ahead and kill the nigga?

Words from The Author

By standing I am a five percenter. I do not consider nor view the black woman in a negative light. It doesn't matter what she may do or be led to do to make herself look bad. No five percenter should be disrespecting her. This is why in my books I present the black woman in a better light than most urban writers.

The honorable Elijah Muhammad once told us that we would never rise any higher if our women aren't raised and that no other people of the world will truly respect us until we learn to respect our woman.

Before I go, know this, not everybody who says they're a Five Percenter is a proper representative of the culture. Some may have yet to grow into wisdom. Some never will, but for the people sincerely looking for the ones who are. Look beneath the surface.

Submission Guideline

Submit the first three chapters of your completed manuscript to ldpsubmissions@gmail.com, subject line: Your book's title. The manuscript must be in a .doc file and sent as an attachment. Document should be in Times New Roman, double spaced and in size 12 font. Also, provide your synopsis and full contact information. If sending multiple submissions, they must each be in a separate email.

Have a story but no way to send it electronically? You can still submit to LDP/Ca$h Presents. Send in the first three chapters, written or typed, of your completed manuscript to:

**LDP: Submissions Dept
Po Box 944
Stockbridge, Ga 30281**

DO NOT send original manuscript. Must be a duplicate.

Provide your synopsis and a cover letter containing your full contact information.

Thanks for considering LDP and Ca$h Presents.

Coming Soon from Lock Down Publications/Ca$h Presents

BOW DOWN TO MY GANGSTA

By **Ca$h**

TORN BETWEEN TWO

By **Coffee**

THE STREETS STAINED MY SOUL **II**

By **Marcellus Allen**

BLOOD OF A BOSS **VI**

SHADOWS OF THE GAME II

By **Askari**

LOYAL TO THE GAME **IV**

By **T.J. & Jelissa**

A DOPEBOY'S PRAYER **II**

By **Eddie "Wolf" Lee**

IF LOVING YOU IS WRONG… **III**

By **Jelissa**

TRUE SAVAGE **VII**

MIDNIGHT CARTEL III

DOPE BOY MAGIC IV

By **Chris Green**

BLAST FOR ME **III**

A SAVAGE DOPEBOY III

CUTTHROAT MAFIA II

By **Ghost**

A HUSTLER'S DECEIT III

KILL ZONE **II**

BAE BELONGS TO ME III

A DOPE BOY'S QUEEN II

By **Aryanna**

COKE KINGS V

KING OF THE TRAP II

By **T.J. Edwards**

GORILLAZ IN THE BAY V

De'Kari

THE STREETS ARE CALLING II

Duquie Wilson

KINGPIN KILLAZ IV

STREET KINGS III

PAID IN BLOOD III

CARTEL KILLAZ IV

DOPE GODS II

Hood Rich

SINS OF A HUSTLA II

ASAD

KINGZ OF THE GAME V

Playa Ray

SLAUGHTER GANG IV

RUTHLESS HEART IV

By Willie Slaughter

THE HEART OF A SAVAGE III

By Jibril Williams

FUK SHYT II

By Blakk Diamond

FEAR MY GANGSTA 5

THE REALEST KILLAS

By Tranay Adams

TRAP GOD II

By Troublesome

YAYO IV

A SHOOTER'S AMBITION III

By S. Allen

GHOST MOB

Stilloan Robinson

KINGPIN DREAMS III

By Paper Boi Rari

CREAM

By Yolanda Moore

SON OF A DOPE FIEND II

By Renta

FOREVER GANGSTA II

GLOCKS ON SATIN SHEETS II

By Adrian Dulan

LOYALTY AIN'T PROMISED II

By Keith Williams

THE PRICE YOU PAY FOR LOVE II

DOPE GIRL MAGIC III

By Destiny Skai

CONFESSIONS OF A GANGSTA II

By Nicholas Lock

I'M NOTHING WITHOUT HIS LOVE II

By Monet Dragun

CAUGHT UP IN THE LIFE III

By Robert Baptiste

LIFE OF A SAVAGE IV

A GANGSTA'S QUR'AN II

By **Romell Tukes**

QUIET MONEY III

THUG LIFE II

By **Trai'Quan**

THE STREETS MADE ME II

By **Larry D. Wright**

THE ULTIMATE SACRIFICE VI

IF YOU CROSSM ME ONCE II

By **Anthony Fields**

THE LIFE OF A HOOD STAR

By Ca$h & Rashia Wilson

Available Now

RESTRAINING ORDER **I & II**

By **CA$H & Coffee**

LOVE KNOWS NO BOUNDARIES **I II & III**

By **Coffee**

RAISED AS A GOON I, II, III & IV

BRED BY THE SLUMS I, II, III

BLAST FOR ME I & II

ROTTEN TO THE CORE I II III

A BRONX TALE I, II, III

DUFFEL BAG CARTEL I II III IV

HEARTLESS GOON I II III IV

A SAVAGE DOPEBOY I II

HEARTLESS GOON I II III

DRUG LORDS I II III

CUTTHROAT MAFIA

By **Ghost**

LAY IT DOWN **I & II**

LAST OF A DYING BREED

BLOOD STAINS OF A SHOTTA I & II III

By **Jamaica**

LOYAL TO THE GAME I II III

LIFE OF SIN I, II III

By **TJ & Jelissa**

BLOODY COMMAS I & II

SKI MASK CARTEL I II & III

KING OF NEW YORK I II,III IV V

RISE TO POWER I II III

COKE KINGS I II III IV

BORN HEARTLESS I II III IV

KING OF THE TRAP

By **T.J. Edwards**

IF LOVING HIM IS WRONG…I & II

LOVE ME EVEN WHEN IT HURTS I II III

By **Jelissa**

WHEN THE STREETS CLAP BACK I & II III

THE HEART OF A SAVAGE I II

By **Jibril Williams**

A DISTINGUISHED THUG STOLE MY HEART I II & III

LOVE SHOULDN'T HURT I II III IV

RENEGADE BOYS I II III IV

PAID IN KARMA I II III

By **Meesha**

A GANGSTER'S CODE I &, II III

A GANGSTER'S SYN I II III

THE SAVAGE LIFE I II III

CHAINED TO THE STREETS I II III

By **J-Blunt**

PUSH IT TO THE LIMIT

Trai'Quan

By **Bre' Hayes**
BLOOD OF A BOSS **I, II, III, IV, V**
SHADOWS OF THE GAME
By **Askari**
THE STREETS BLEED MURDER **I, II & III**
THE HEART OF A GANGSTA I II& III
By **Jerry Jackson**
CUM FOR ME I II III IV V
An **LDP Erotica Collaboration**
BRIDE OF A HUSTLA **I II & II**
THE FETTI GIRLS **I, II& III**
CORRUPTED BY A GANGSTA I, II III, IV
BLINDED BY HIS LOVE
THE PRICE YOU PAY FOR LOVE
DOPE GIRL MAGIC I II
By **Destiny Skai**
WHEN A GOOD GIRL GOES BAD
By **Adrienne**
THE COST OF LOYALTY I II III
By Kweli
A GANGSTER'S REVENGE **I II III & IV**
THE BOSS MAN'S DAUGHTERS I II III IV V
A SAVAGE LOVE **I & II**
BAE BELONGS TO ME I II
A HUSTLER'S DECEIT I, II, III
WHAT BAD BITCHES DO I, II, III
SOUL OF A MONSTER I II III
KILL ZONE
A DOPE BOY'S QUEEN
By **Aryanna**

174

A KINGPIN'S AMBITON
A KINGPIN'S AMBITION **II**
I MURDER FOR THE DOUGH
By **Ambitious**
TRUE SAVAGE I II III IV V VI
DOPE BOY MAGIC I, II, III
MIDNIGHT CARTEL I II
By **Chris Green**
A DOPEBOY'S PRAYER
By **Eddie "Wolf" Lee**
THE KING CARTEL **I, II & III**
By **Frank Gresham**
THESE NIGGAS AIN'T LOYAL **I, II & III**
By **Nikki Tee**
GANGSTA SHYT **I II &III**
By **CATO**
THE ULTIMATE BETRAYAL
By **Phoenix**
BOSS'N UP **I , II & III**
By **Royal Nicole**
I LOVE YOU TO DEATH
By Destiny J
I RIDE FOR MY HITTA
I STILL RIDE FOR MY HITTA
By **Misty Holt**
LOVE & CHASIN' PAPER
By **Qay Crockett**
TO DIE IN VAIN
SINS OF A HUSTLA
By **ASAD**

BROOKLYN HUSTLAZ

By **Boogsy Morina**

BROOKLYN ON LOCK I & II

By **Sonovia**

GANGSTA CITY

By **Teddy Duke**

A DRUG KING AND HIS DIAMOND I & II III

A DOPEMAN'S RICHES

HER MAN, MINE'S TOO I, II

CASH MONEY HO'S

By Nicole Goosby

TRAPHOUSE KING **I II & III**

KINGPIN KILLAZ I II III

STREET KINGS I II

PAID IN BLOOD **I II**

CARTEL KILLAZ I II III

DOPE GODS

By **Hood Rich**

LIPSTICK KILLAH **I, II, III**

CRIME OF PASSION I II & III

By **Mimi**

STEADY MOBBN' **I, II, III**

THE STREETS STAINED MY SOUL

By **Marcellus Allen**

WHO SHOT YA **I, II, III**

SON OF A DOPE FIEND

Renta

GORILLAZ IN THE BAY **I II III IV**

TEARS OF A GANGSTA I II

DE'KARI

Thug Life

TRIGGADALE I II III

Elijah R. Freeman

GOD BLESS THE TRAPPERS I, II, III

THESE SCANDALOUS STREETS I, II, III

FEAR MY GANGSTA I, II, III IV

THESE STREETS DON'T LOVE NOBODY I, II

BURY ME A G I, II, III, IV, V

A GANGSTA'S EMPIRE I, II, III, IV

THE DOPEMAN'S BODYGAURD I II

Tranay Adams

THE STREETS ARE CALLING

Duquie Wilson

MARRIED TO A BOSS... I II III

By Destiny Skai & Chris Green

KINGZ OF THE GAME I II III IV

Playa Ray

SLAUGHTER GANG I II III

RUTHLESS HEART I II III

By Willie Slaughter

FUK SHYT

By Blakk Diamond

DON'T F#CK WITH MY HEART I II

By Linnea

ADDICTED TO THE DRAMA I II III

By Jamila

YAYO I II III

A SHOOTER'S AMBITION I II

By S. Allen

TRAP GOD

By Troublesome

FOREVER GANGSTA

GLOCKS ON SATIN SHEETS

By Adrian Dulan

TOE TAGZ I II III

By Ah'Million

KINGPIN DREAMS I II

By Paper Boi Rari

CONFESSIONS OF A GANGSTA

By Nicholas Lock

I'M NOTHING WITHOUT HIS LOVE

By Monet Dragun

CAUGHT UP IN THE LIFE I II

By Robert Baptiste

NEW TO THE GAME I II III

By **Malik D. Rice**

LIFE OF A SAVAGE I II III

A GANGSTA'S QUR'AN

By **Romell Tukes**

LOYALTY AIN'T PROMISED

By Keith Williams

QUIET MONEY I II

THUG LIFE

By **Trai'Quan**

THE STREETS MADE ME

By **Larry D. Wright**

THE ULTIMATE SACRIFICE I, II, III, IV, V

KHADIFI

IF YOU CROSS ME ONCE

By **Anthony Fields**

THE LIFE OF A HOOD STAR

Thug Life

By Ca$h & Rashia Wilson

Trai'Quan

BOOKS BY LDP'S CEO, CA$H

TRUST IN NO MAN

TRUST IN NO MAN 2

TRUST IN NO MAN 3

BONDED BY BLOOD

SHORTY GOT A THUG

THUGS CRY

THUGS CRY 2

THUGS CRY 3

TRUST NO BITCH

TRUST NO BITCH 2

TRUST NO BITCH 3

TIL MY CASKET DROPS

RESTRAINING ORDER

RESTRAINING ORDER 2

IN LOVE WITH A CONVICT

LIFE OF A HOOD STAR

Coming Soon

BONDED BY BLOOD 2

BOW DOWN TO MY GANGSTA

Thug Life

CPSIA information can be obtained
at www.ICGtesting.com
Printed in the USA
LVHW050444161020
668921LV00012B/1457